YORK NOTES

General Editors: Professor A.N. Jeffares (Uni~~~~~~~
of Stirling) & Professor Suheil Bushrui (A~~~~~~~~
University of Beirut)

Chinua A~~~~

THINGS
FALL APART

Notes by T.A. Dunn

MA PH D (EDINBURGH)

LONGMAN
YORK PRESS

Extracts from *Things Fall Apart* by Chinua Achebe are
reprinted by kind permission of William Heinemann Limited
© Chinua Achebe 1958.

YORK PRESS
Immeuble Esseily, Place Riad Solh, Beirut

LONGMAN GROUP LIMITED
Longman House, Burnt Mill, Harlow,
Essex CM20 2JE, England
Associated companies, branches and representatives
throughout the world

© Librairie du Liban 1981

All rights reserved; no part of this publication may be reproduced,
stored in a retrieval system, or transmitted in any form or by any
means, electronic, mechanical, photocopying, recording, or otherwise,
without either the prior written permission of the Publishers or a
licence permitting restricted copying in the United Kingdom issued by
the Copyright Licensing Agency Ltd, 90 Tottenham Court Road, London W1P 9HE.

First published 1981
Tenth impression 1994

ISBN 0-582-02312-2

Produced by Longman Singapore Publishers Pte Ltd
Printed in Singapore

Contents

Part 1

Introduction

Life of Chinua Achebe

Chinua Achebe is the leading, and certainly the best-known, writer of
fiction in black Africa. His novels are read all over the English-speaking
world and are studied in universities and for school examinations in
Africa, Britain, North America and even in Australia, and in his posi-
tions as founding editor of Heinemann's 'African Writers Series' and
editor of the magazine *Okeke*, as well as a prominent lecturer and
broadcaster, his influence on the development of African literature in
English has been considerable.

He was born in Ogidi, to the north-east of Onitsha in Eastern Nigeria,
in 1930, and was the fifth of the six children of Isaiah Okafor Achebe,
one of the early Ibo converts to Christianity who was evangelist and
teacher in the Church Missionary Society's village school. Chinua
attended his father's school and, having started to learn English at about
the age of eight, went on to Government College, Umuahia, in 1944. In
1948 he entered University College, Ibadan—at that time in special
relationship with the University of London—with a scholarship to
study medicine. After a year he switched to literature and was one of
Ibadan's first graduates in 1953. At that time, the syllabus that he followed in English literature was very much the same as that which would
have been followed by an undergraduate in Britain, since the newly
established colleges in the overseas territories were then very much
carbon copies of the traditional British universities and had not yet
started the process of change and decolonisation that was to turn them
into the fully-fledged and free institutions, adjusted to the needs of
independent nations, that they have since become. One advantage of
this, from the point of view of Achebe as a novelist, was that he was
immediately introduced to the mainstream of the English novel and to
its close critical study. In particular, he was introduced to the complex
and carefully constructed masterpieces of Joseph Conrad (1857–1924),
the Polish author who chose to write his novels in English, and to a
range of English writers who had written about Africa from the outside.
In addition, he was awakened to the power of fiction for expressing the
most profound ideas of human experience and for giving voice to the
deepest feelings of the individual human spirit. At the same time his
interest in the history of Nigeria had grown, so it is not surprising that

when he turned to storytelling he should turn as one not only fully informed in the analysis of English fiction but also as one determined to express through this means the spirit of his people and write about Africa from the inside.

After teaching for a few months, he joined the Nigerian Broadcasting Corporation in 1954 as a Talks Producer and rose, by way of being Head of the Talks Section (1957) and Controller, Eastern Region (1959), to become Director of External Services in 1961. His job took him on long journeys about Nigeria and, as he drove, his mind was busy reviewing the history and life of his people and casting this mass of unique material in the classical fictional moulds he had studied at university. This resulted, in 1958, in the publication of his first novel, *Things Fall Apart*. It was an immediate success and won for him the Margaret Wrong Prize. *No Longer At Ease* was published in 1960 and won the Nigerian National Trophy. *Arrow of God* came out in 1964 and made him the first recipient of the *New Statesman* Jock Campbell Award, and his fourth, and so far his last, novel, *A Man of the People*, appeared in 1966.

With the massacre of the Ibos in Northern Nigeria in 1966 and the beginning of the Nigerian troubles, he resigned from the Broadcasting Corporation and moved back to Eastern Nigeria. There, when the region declared itself independent under the name of Biafra, he threw in his lot with his fellow-Ibos during the civil war. Since the war he has concentrated on rebuilding the University of Nigeria, Nssuka, where he now teaches, but he taught for two years in the United States, at the University of Massachusetts in Amherst and at the University of Connecticut.

It is clear to those who know him that the Biafran conflict and his experiences then have had a profound effect on Achebe, and it seems reasonable to guess that ultimately these will show in a fifth novel. Some of the stories in *Girls at War* (1971), a collection of short stories which includes some earlier work, and some of the poems in *Beware Soul Brother* (1972) concern the war, as do several of the essays in his most recent collection *Morning Yet on Creation Day* (1975). Even if another novel does not deal directly with that tragic conflict, it would be impossible for a writer of Achebe's sensitivity to avoid showing how such an experience has changed his attitude to life.

As will be apparent to anyone who reads his novels, Achebe sets great importance on family life and relationships. It is clear that he had a particularly happy and warm upbringing himself and he is most concerned to create the same atmosphere for his own children. It is not surprising, therefore, that one of his works (albeit not very well known to critics) has been *Chike and the River* (Cambridge University Press, 1966), an adventure story for children.

As well as prizes for his books, Achebe has received many honours and they have often brought with them the possibility for travelling widely all over the world. He gained a Rockefeller Grant in 1960, and a UNESCO travel award in 1963. In 1974 he was awarded a Fellowship of the Modern Languages Association of America and Honorary Doctorates in both the Universities of Stirling and Southampton; and in 1975 he was made the second recipient of the Scottish Arts Council's Neil Gunn Fellowship, following one Nobel prizewinner, Heinrich Böll (1973), and preceding another, Saul Bellow (1977). That is the company he keeps—that of the most sophisticated writers in the world—this son of a small Nigerian village, grandson of a simple Ibo tribesman.

Achebe's work

The main body of Achebe's work rests in the four novels—*Things Fall Apart* (1958), *No Longer At Ease* (1960), *Arrow of God* (1964) and *A Man of the People* (1966). These Notes are concerned only with the first of these, but it is worthy of remark that there are ways in which these novels are related to one another and to the author's life.

Things Fall Apart recounts events that, allegedly, took place at about the time of his grandfather; his grandfather had a son (Achebe's father) who was converted to Christianity under the name of Isaiah. We will recall that Okonkwo's son, Nwoye, in *Things Fall Apart*, is also converted to Christianity, and baptised Isaac. And in *No Longer At Ease*, which some people see as the sequel to the earlier novel, the chief character, Obi Okonkwo, is Okonkwo's grandson, the son of Nwoye who is now a retired church schoolteacher living in Umuofia—a position identical to that of Achebe's father. There, however, the main bones of autobiography stop, for Obi Okonkwo is not in any way like Achebe himself. Achebe has, in fact, taken merely the main circumstances of his own family over three critical generations and used them as the peg on which to hang his stories. And Okonkwo is no more like Achebe's grandfather than Obi Okonkwo is like Achebe himself. In fact, his grandfather and grandmother died young and Isaiah Achebe was brought up by his mother's father—one further generation back in the family history. What Achebe has done, of course, is to flesh out his stories with what in his childhood he was told of the events, circumstances and way of life of the past and with the legends of his people that he heard from the lips of his mother and his elder sister.

Achebe has said that originally he had considered writing three novels dealing with the recent history of his people and his country. The first, illustrating the conflicts arising with the arrival of the Europeans, is *Things Fall Apart*. The second was to exhibit the problems facing the generation of Okonkwo's son, Nwoye. This he did not write. The third was to illustrate the Nigeria of the late-1950s, of Okonkwo's grandson, Obi: this is his second published novel, *No Longer At Ease*.

The reason he never wrote the second novel is not altogether clear. It is true that a man can find it difficult to write a novel about his own father, a man whom he has actually known and—in Achebe's case at least—loved. He has told us himself that the reason he never wrote the middle story of the three he had originally projected was that he suddenly realised that he knew little about his own grandfather. The man he had been writing about, with whose times he had been involved, was in reality his father's grandfather, a member of a still older generation. That is why the events of *Things Fall Apart* seem to be coming from much further back than the mere turn of the century, since, although Achebe had plenty of experience of the traditional, non-Christian way of life in his own childhood, he was really re-creating the world and times of his great-grandfather, Udo Osinyi.

No Longer At Ease tells the story of young Obi Okonkwo who, having been educated in the United Kingdom, returns to Nigeria to take up a post in the Civil Service in Lagos. Lagos is a cosmopolitan city in a flux and ferment in which the traditional values of caring and kinship, exemplified by the old Umuofia, are at odds with the values of acquisitive contemporary society which are largely materialistic and selfish. In such a life young Obi's high ideals do not stand much chance of surviving. His determination to stamp out corruption cannot withstand the Umuofian view that the home community that paid to educate one of its sons to place him in government service ought thereby to benefit. His own impatience with traditional order in wishing to marry a member of the prohibited *osu* caste brings him inevitably into conflict with his family and people. Thus he cannot fit into either world, succumbs to bribery and ends in prison.

As a novel it has nothing of the scale and stature of *Things Fall Apart*. Okonkwo is a hero we can admire: Obi is merely a young man with whom we can sympathise. The events display the muddled dilemmas in which such a man is placed, largely through his own folly. The dilemmas are real enough, but most of them could have been solved by a sympathetic bank manager and could have been avoided by a man of more moral fibre. Solutions are not offered. The Europeans are, one must suppose, intended to be satirical presentations but are mere paste-board characters, and one is forced to wonder whether, if an African novelist is so bad at presenting Europeans, it is perhaps likely that Europeans are just as unsuccessful when they try to depict Africans. Yet the fact remains that this is a novel that is tremendously popular with young West Africans, who are those best fitted to understand Obi's problems, and thus, since Achebe sees African readers as his main market, it must be accounted a success.

Arrow of God, Achebe's third novel, is very different from the two earlier works, both in scale and in treatment, and in it he confirms himself as a writer of major stature, as a true novelist and not merely a happy literary accident. The novel goes back almost to the period of *Things Fall Apart* to deal more specifically with the struggle between Christianity and the old religion, which is symbolised as the Python, the creative force of the Ibo faith; and in it he displays both maturity and experience, producing a work of high artistry and intelligent selfconsciousness. It concerns Ezeulu, priest of the god Ulu, and his struggle to assert the primacy of the cult of his god over other gods. The situation is complicated not only by the new Christian faith but also, more significantly, by deep rifts and divisions of faith within the Ibo people, and, much more than in Achebe's other books, it depends upon the ambiguous complexity of the principal character. Ezeulu's unbending nature brings about his own ruin, disaster to his followers and a strengthening of his enemies—in particular the Christians. It is Achebe's most difficult book and is a masterpiece quite different in kind from *Things Fall Apart*.

In the two novels of the past Achebe seems perfectly at home in his task of reconciling himself to his ancestors and of presenting to his fellow-Africans a pre-colonial past in which they could take pride, producing works that are tragic in intensity and epic in scale. In the two novels dealing with the present he is not so successful—as if his involvement with, and nearness to, the events of today had clouded the clarity and objectivity of his vision. *No Longer At Ease* introduces an uneasily satirical tone and his last novel, *A Man of the People*, is deliberately and bitterly satirical.

When it was published in 1966, *A Man of the People* was seen as prophetic of the political disasters in Nigeria that so soon followed; and, indeed, a political disaster was an inevitable outcome of the situation Achebe so bitterly describes. The novel is a satirical farce about the way in which politicians so corruptly manipulate the power that had been left to them by the departed imperial master. Odili, the young schoolmaster through whom the story is presented, confronts the corrupt politician, Nanga, ostensibly on political principle but actually in rivalry over a woman. In the end we can see Odili as every bit as cynical and self-seeking as Nanga. None of the principal characters is admirable in any way and there are those who find the book too bitter and too angry. If Achebe ever were to write a novel on the Biafran tragedy this would be the tone against which he would have to guard. If he could introduce the tragic objectivity that is the striking feature of *Things Fall Apart* and *Arrow of God* then he would indeed produce another masterpiece.

Thirty of Achebe's poems are published in *Beware Soul Brother*

(1972), which is a revised and enlarged edition of a volume published the previous year in Nigeria. *Morning Yet on Creation Day* (1975) is a collection of fifteen lectures and essays written between 1961 and 1974, more than half of them dating from after the publication of his last novel. All of them are both interesting and of relevance to his work, but of particular interest to students are the autobiographical 'Named for Victoria, Queen of England' (pp.65–70) and the account of Ibo beliefs in '*Chi* in Igbo Cosmology' (pp.93–103).

The background of the novel

The Ibo people are a large nation of related tribes, now numbering around eleven million people, sharing a common language, common beliefs and traditions and a common social structure. In English, both they and their language are known as 'Ibo', but they prefer themselves to use the form 'Igbo'. They inhabit a very large forest area of inland south-eastern Nigeria, between the Niger and the Cross Rivers, and though, in past history, they were a peaceful, agricultural people, their intelligence and capacity for hard work and their high regard for education caused them to spread out over Nigeria as traders, teachers and professional men with the economic development that followed the settlement of the country in the first half of the twentieth century.

They were never organised as a 'nation' in the modern political sense but, based upon the extended family and elaborate kinship and clan relationships, were organised in small villages or groups of villages, getting along with neighbouring villages through a system of agreements, petty squabbles and settlements that had evolved throughout the centuries. *Things Fall Apart* shows how these arrangements worked, as well as the various social rituals engaged in by the Ibos that were appropriate to their way of life. It should be made clear, however, that they were organised on democratic and republican lines, that a man was esteemed for himself, his achievements and his value to the community and not for what his father was. They settled everything political by argument and discussion, dearly loved the ritual of speeches, for or against any side, liberally larded with proverbs, and thus were regarded as highly argumentative individualists. They were honest, but always drove a hard bargain. Unlike the African peoples further west along the Guinea coast, they inherited from the father's side and the creative force of their religion was the Sun (male) rather than the Moon (female).

Though most of them now are either Christians or agnostics, the traditional religion of the Ibo people was one in which there were a great many gods under one great God, Chukwu, in which ancestor-worship and reincarnation featured and in which the otherworld, inhabited by the gods and the dead, ran parallel to and interpenetrated the everyday

world of present reality. The priests and priestesses interpret\
otherworld to mortals, often becoming 'possessed' by the spirit ol
god or oracle, and the gods themselves could visit this world in the ɡᵤɪse
of masked dancers, called *egwugwu*, who wore elaborate disguises of
raffia, straw and carved wooden heads. Simple people might believe
that these really were the gods, but those in the know were aware that
they were really humans in disguise. Nevertheless, the tribesman himself knew that his ordinary, everyday self was one thing and that when
he was *egwugwu* he was another. In a sense, as with the priests and
priestesses, he was a vehicle for the god. In addition, each man had a
personal god or *chi* that is his spiritual other-self—part soul, part
personal god and part fate. However, all the complexities of the Ibo
faith are either explained by Achebe in the novel or can easily be deduced
from what he says about them.

Things Fall Apart is, of course, about the Ibos and their position towards the end of the nineteenth century when faced with the first European penetration of their country, bringing with it a new religion, new
ideas and a money-based economy. But the dilemmas faced by the Ibos
were those that confronted many peoples all over Africa and, indeed,
in other parts of the world. For the political structure of modern Africa
was created by act of the super-powers who divided it up into units that
often paid little regard to the natural social and language groupings of
the peoples who were colonised. Their motives were nominally those of
evangelism and of 'bringing light' to the dark places of the world, but
were in reality motives of trade. The results of this action are still being
lived with today. Yet, however arrogant and misguided, or even wicked,
the motives of the nineteenth-century colonisers may seem to us today,
the fact remains that the individuals who were engaged in this enter-
prise—administrators, teachers, doctors, missionaries and traders—
often worked for the highest motives and were men of the highest calibre.
One interesting thing about Achebe is that he does not condemn these
men, as he could so easily have done, any more than he presents pre-
colonial Africa as a Garden of Eden. In this story, simple, strong and
epic, he presents things as they were, without condemnation and only
occasionally with the wryest of ironic comments, so that we can see for
ourselves the tragedy of a human being caught up in circumstances of
history over which he has no control.

A note on the text

Things Fall Apart was first published in 1958 by Heinemann, London,
as No. 1 of their 'African Writers Series', of which Achebe is founding
editor, and has been constantly available since then. The text has not
been revised but it has been reset several times. Thus the page numbers

do not correspond in the various editions. The edition currently available was first published in 1967 and has the addition of a brief biographical note, a glossary of Ibo words and phrases and four line-drawings by Uche Okeke.

Several shortened versions designed for young schoolchildren are also available. These should not be used by those studying the novel. There is also a 'Students' Edition', with an Introduction and Notes by Aigboji Higo, which was published by Heinemann in 1965.

Part 2

Summaries
of THINGS FALL APART

A general summary

Things Fall Apart is a novel of twenty-five short chapters, divided into three parts—Chapters 1–13, 14–19 and 20–25.

The title is taken from a poem called 'The Second Coming' by the Irish poet W.B. Yeats (1865–1939), in which he laments the passing of order and innocence from the world and fears that the changes that are taking place may not be for the best. In the poem, Yeats says:

Things fall apart; the centre cannot hold;
Mere anarchy is loosed upon the world,
The blood-dimmed tide is loosed, and everywhere
The ceremony of innocence is drowned.

It can be seen immediately how appropriate this title is for this novel, which describes the change that comes over an old and firmly established society and social structure under the impact of new, different and more advanced ideas from outside.

The novel is set in Ibo-land towards the end of the nineteenth century, when Europeans were just beginning to penetrate inland in West Africa. Ibo-land is now a part of the Federal Republic of Nigeria and lies on the other side of the Niger River in the east of that great country. In the late 1960s the Ibo-speaking peoples attempted to secede from the Federation under the name of Biafra, and the tragic civil war that followed cost many lives. Now the country is peaceful and the Ibo people are assimilated with various of the eastern Nigerian states. At the time of the novel, however, there was no idea of nationhood or the modern state in West Africa, and 'Ibo-land' is merely the convenient name we give to that large area settled by a people who all spoke the same language, Ibo, and who shared the same social structure and cultural and religious ideas. They were organised into groups of related villages in a basically democratic system, engaged in simple subsistence farming, and their lives were lived within a highly formalised framework of social relationships and of primitive, animistic religion in which respect for ancestors and magic played a very large part.

Part One of the novel shows us just such a community, Umuofia, a group of nine related villages, in the period just before the arrival of the white man. Of course, the West African coast—particularly the mouth of the Niger and the Calabar Rivers—had been visited, and even settled, by Europeans for a long time, and certain importations (for example, some of the food crops and gunpowder and muskets) had penetrated inland; but none of the villagers of Umuofia had ever seen a white man and all their knowledge of them was through distant tales of slave-trading exploits.

We learn of the life of Umuofia at this period through following the life of Okonkwo, one of its prominent citizens, in a series of brief, episodic chapters. Though there is, of course, a 'story' about Okonkwo, and many of the episodes are designed to reveal his character, the main concern of Part One is, by using Okonkwo, to give us a detailed picture of the way of life of this people as it had remained unchanged for many generations.

Thus we learn of their crops and how they are planted, of their disputes and how they are settled, of their elaborate social rituals and the ceremonies with which the high-spots of their lives—harvests, marriages, and the like—are celebrated, and also of their highly formalised modes of address and discussion. Most of all, we learn of the way in which their everyday lives are interpenetrated with the otherworld of magic and mystery and of the part played in their lives by superstition and the witch-doctors. Yet the picture given is not of an unhappy society. It is stable, governed by tradition and custom, and if some of their practices may seem ignorant or barbaric to us today, these people lived a life that was strong and firmly knit, and that had its own considerable virtues and values: every man knew his place and what was expected of him and subscribed to a generally accepted system of beliefs.

Okonkwo is very much a man of this old order. He is courageous and brave, a fearless fighter and highly respected in his clan; and he is a strong believer in traditional faith and practices. Moreover, he is hard-working and determined to make a successful life, very unlike his father, Unoka, who had been more fond of music and merrymaking than of hard work and of gaining the respect of his fellows. Thus, when there is a dispute with a neighbouring village, it is Okonkwo who is sent as ambassador and who becomes the guardian of the hostage, Ikemefuna, who is given to the tribe by way of reparations.

Okonkwo is a man who prefers doing things to being inactive, who prefers manly sports such as wrestling to sitting around feasting. When he has nothing to do he is very irritable and treats his wives and children harshly. Indeed, he is always very stern with them. His son, Nwoye, in particular, is a disappointment to Okonkwo, since he sees him like his own father, but he grows increasingly fond of the hostage, Ikemefuna. It comes as a shock to him, therefore, when one of the elders tells him that the gods have decreed that Ikemefuna is to be sacrificed. By a ruse, Ikemefuna is taken out into the bush and when, without warning, one of the men strikes him, he runs towards Okonkwo whom he sees as his father. There is a critical moment where Okonkwo is torn between his feelings for the boy and his strong sense of duty to the gods, but the latter sense prevails and he strikes Ikemefuna down. In this way we are shown how the traditional ways can often be very brutal; particularly affected by the brutality of this incident is Okonkwo's more gentle-natured son, Nwoye.

In the remaining chapters of Part One more of the customs of Umuofia are displayed. We see traditional justice being exercised in the settlement of a matrimonial dispute by the assembled elders and the *egwugwu* (masked representatives of the spirits), and Okonkwo takes part in the negotiations for the marriage of his friend Obierika, the whole village participating in the wedding-feast when it eventually takes place. In addition, we learn of Okonkwo's love for his young daughter, Ezinma, in an incident in which the priestess of the Oracle carries her off in the night to her cave, closely followed by Okonkwo and her mother who wait outside until she is safely returned. At another point she is cured of malaria by Okonkwo, who uses a traditional herbal recipe as a medicine.

The climax of Part One comes in Chapter 13. At the funeral of one of the elders of the village, Okonkwo's gun explodes, killing the young son of the dead man. To be responsible for the killing of a fellow-tribesman is a major crime and carries with it the automatic penalty of exile. Since the killing was an accident, Okonkwo's exile is to be for seven years, and, together with his wives and children, he has to leave for his mother's village of Mbanta. Thus the end of Part One brings to an end Okonkwo's period of settled life in Umuofia and rudely interrupts his hitherto successful career among his clansmen. When he returns to it again both it and his life will have changed.

Part Two of the novel (Chapters 14–19) covers Okonkwo's years of exile in Mbanta. During his exile, he is visited by his friend, Obierika, who has been looking after his affairs in Umuofia. From him he learns of how the first white man had arrived in one of the villages and been killed and of how the white men had exacted vengeance for his death by massacring the villagers. Two years later Obierika comes to visit him again. White missionaries have arrived in the district and he has seen Okonkwo's son, Nwoye, amongst the converts. Most of the remainder of this part shows how the missionaries had come to Mbanta and how their influence had spread, converting first of all the outcasts or those who were otherwise dissatisfied with Ibo society and those who, like Nwoye, felt that the new religion had something to offer them. The spread of Christianity threatens the peace of the land, and this threat leads to the establishment of courts and the white man's rule of law and order.

Now Okonkwo is estranged from his son. Everything he believed in and the society in which he held an honourable place is threatened, and his natural reaction is to fight in defence of the old order and to drive the white men out by violence. But before he leaves Mbanta to return in, as he thinks, triumph to Umuofia at the end of his period of exile, he holds a great feast for his kinsfolk—a final demonstration of the strengths of the old, the traditional way of life.

Part Three (Chapters 20-5) brings the final, tragic phase of Okonkwo's story. Returned to Umuofia, he finds that things have indeed changed. A court has been established as well as a mission-school and hospital run by a far-sighted missionary who tries to understand the Ibos and sees that a head-on collision with their culture will be fruitless. When he leaves and is replaced by a more narrow-minded man, trouble is inevitable. When one of the more rabid converts commits the unpardonable crime of unmasking an *egwugwu* during a traditional ceremony, Umuofia explodes and the mission-church is burnt to the ground by the irate populace.

Six of the leading citizens, including Okonkwo, are called to the court-house, where they are arrested, clapped in chains and the community fined heavily for their misdemeanour. During their detention they are beaten and maltreated by the District Commissioner's men, who are Ibos from distant tribes. On their release a great assembly of the villagers takes place to discuss what is to be done, and when the Commissioner's men arrive to stop the meeting, Okonkwo, who has been arguing for violent action, kills one of the messengers. The following day, when men arrive to arrest Okonkwo, they find that he has hanged himself, having preferred the shameful course of taking his own life to submitting to the white man's justice.

Detailed summaries

Part One, Chapter 1

Okonkwo, who is now in his forties, is a man of tremendous reputation in the nine villages of Umuofia, famous for his strength and courage and for his prowess as a fighter. When he was only eighteen he defeated Amalinze the Cat in a wrestling-match, and since that victory his reputation has grown and increased. He is a champion wrestler, has fought bravely in two inter-tribal wars, and has become a wealthy farmer with three wives and two barns full of yams.

His father, Unoka, who had died ten years before the story begins, had been a very different kind of man. He was lazy, never saved any money and liked best of all playing the flute, drinking and merrymaking.

As a grown man he had been a failure, unable to provide for his wife and children and always borrowing money which he could not repay. As an example of this, we are shown how Unoka deals with a friend, Okoye, to whom he owes money, and it is clear from this scene that Unoka is a gentle, persuasive man, skilled at adorning his conversation with the proverbs beloved by the Ibos, a man who loves the softer and more 'feminine' things in life, such as music and dancing. These qualities were not valued by the Ibo society of the time, as were the stern qualities displayed by his son, Okonkwo.

Now, although his father had been a waster, Okonkwo had, by his own efforts, made himself one of the most important men in his village of Umuofia.

NOTES AND GLOSSARY:

harmattan:	the dry, dusty wind that blows south from the Sahara in January
gourd:	the hard skin of a round fruit, used as a drinking-vessel
palm-wine:	an intoxicating drink made by fermenting the sap of the oil-palm
cowries:	a type of sea-shell, formerly used as money in West Africa
egwugwu:	a masked dancer who impersonates a spirit in Ibo rituals
kite:	a large scavenging bird of the hawk kind
kola:	the nut of a West African tree, slightly narcotic in effect, used in Ibo social rituals, particularly, as here, in greeting a guest
ekwe, udu, ogene:	drums and gongs, used in Ibo music
yams:	a large root-crop which is a staple diet in West Africa
palm-oil:	oil pressed from palm-nuts, used in West African cooking

Chapter 2

A woman from Umuofia has been killed in the neighbouring village of Mbaino, and the members of the tribe, summoned by the town-crier, gather in the village square to hear an account of the incident. They agree to send Okonkwo as their ambassador to Mbaino to find out whether the offending villagers were prepared to go to war over the matter or if they would pay, by way of compensation to Umuofia, one youth and one maiden. Such is the warlike reputation of Umuofia, known to be backed up by a powerful War Spirit, that the people of

Mbaino readily agree to a peaceful settlement. In these negotiations Okonkwo plays the main part, and on his return the elders make him the guardian of the male hostage, Ikemefuna.

Throughout this episode, Okonkwo's proud and strong nature is stressed, his status within his tribe and the harsh way in which he rules his family. He seems a brave, even cruel, man, but, in reality, his life is ruled by fear of weakness and failure, of becoming a good-for-nothing laughing-stock like his father. We learn more of his wealth and of his son, Nwoye, who, he is afraid, is turning out to be an idler. We also learn of how the whole life of the tribe is governed by magic and superstition.

NOTES AND GLOSSARY:

kwenu:	hail! (a shout of greeting or approval)
medicine:	a word used to apply to any magic or *juju*: sometimes it is a shrine or a sacred object and sometimes it is the spell or ritual associated with that particular shrine or form of worship
Oracle:	a sacred shrine whose priest makes inspired pronouncements of divine warning or advice to the tribe
ndichie:	elders of the tribe
agbala:	a woman; used contemptuously of a man of no significance, with no title
compound:	the walled living-area of a family within which they erect their sleeping-huts and food-stores

Chapter 3

Unoka's life had been dogged by misfortune and he made a miserable end. Once, on visiting the Oracle, he had been told clearly that the fault was within himself, in that he never exerted himself on his own behalf and did not work hard enough. So Okonkwo started with no advantages and has had to exert himself mightily to build up his fortune. This he has succeeded in doing, driven on in his tremendous efforts by the fear of being a failure, like his father. An example is given of how he had made his way when he was young by clearing a farm and planting the seed of a wealthy man, Nwakibie, in return for some of the produce. As well, this scene shows the elaborate social rituals and proverb-laden forms of address used by the Ibo. That particular year had been one of drought and crop-failure, but Okonkwo had worked hard and not allowed this failure to break his spirit. Gradually a picture is being built up of Okonkwo's manly determination, courage and capacity for hard work, as opposed to his father's weakness.

NOTES AND GLOSSARY:

bush:	uncultivated land, jungle
chi:	personal god
obi:	the main hut in a compound, used by the head of the family
tapper:	one who draws off the sap from the oil-palm for making palm-wine
iroko:	a large West African hardwood tree
share-cropping:	clearing and working a farm but planting another man's seed in return for a share of the produce
sisal:	a long-bladed plant whose dried leaves are used like raffia or to make ropes
market weeks:	the weeks were marked by market-days, which came round every four days

Chapter 4

Although Okonkwo is bold and adventurous, he is also arrogant and proud, caring little for others' feelings and accounting any softness as weakness. He is harsh to his family, being particularly stern to his son, Nwoye, and to the unhappy and homesick Ikemefuna. He seems not to care for either man or god. For example, during the Week of Peace, an annual festival during which violent action is forbidden, he beats one of his wives for neglecting her duty and is fined by the priest, but though he is inwardly repentant his pride will not let him show others that he cares.

After the Week of Peace is the time for planting the yams, and we see with what care Okonkwo carries out the various operations, taking the boys to task for not doing things properly. Yet, in spite of himself, he is growing attached to Ikemefuna, who is at last settling down, while the two boys are becoming fast friends.

NOTES AND GLOSSARY:

palm-kernels:	the seeds of the oil-palm which have to be cracked before the oil is pressed out of them
nso-ani:	a religious offence, a sin

Chapter 5

Each year in Umuofia, when the yams are ready to be harvested, a great festival is held, called the Feast of the New Yam. It marks the beginning of the period of plentiful food, between harvesting and the next planting, when there is no work to be done in the fields, and it is celebrated with feasting, drumming and wrestling. Okonkwo, being a man of action, does not like such periods of inactivity, and he loses his temper with his family, even going so far as firing his rusty old gun at one of his wives. Fortunately, he does no harm and the feast in Okonkwo's house proceeds, attended by his many relatives.

The second day of the feast is the day of a wrestling-contest between the neighbouring villages, an event that appeals much more to Okonkwo. But first we see something of the domestic arrangements of his household, how food is prepared by his wives and his little daughter, Ezinma, and how the various dishes are served to Okonkwo. All this takes place against a background of gathering excitement as the sound of the drums comes from the village square where the wrestling is to take place.

NOTES AND GLOSSARY:

calabashes:	drinking-vessels made of gourds
mortar:	vessel used for pounding up food, usually of wood
foo-foo:	boiled, pounded-up yam, used as a staple food in West Africa; nowadays this is more often made from pounded cassava-root
cam wood:	red dye made from a wood, used for body-painting
inyanga:	showing off, posturing in an impertinent way

Chapter 6

The wrestling-match is not a simple sporting contest but is a ritual event, taking place in front of the sacred silk-cotton tree and accompanied by drummers who, when they are drumming, are no longer ordinary human beings but are in some sense 'possessed' by the sacred spirit. In the same way Chielo, to whom Ekwefi tells the story of how Okonkwo had fired his gun at her, seems one person in her ordinary life and quite a different one when she is the priestess of the Oracle.

So the wrestling proceeds, by ordered formality, until Ikezue and Okafo, the two acknowledged champions, meet and, after a hard fight, Okafo is the winner. The celebrations have risen to a crescendo of excitement when the drums have become 'the very heart-beat of the people' and, singing a song of victory, the crowd then bears the winner home.

NOTES AND GLOSSARY:

ilo:	the village square
perhaps she has come to stay:	since many children died in infancy it was thought to be unlucky and tempting the evil spirits to think that a child was here to stay in this world until it was past the dangerous period of childhood

Chapter 7

Three years have passed. Ikemefuna has settled down in Okonkwo's household and is having a good influence upon Nwoye who is growing up and becoming closer to his father. Yet, although he pretends to enjoy his father's warlike stories, in his heart he prefers the gentler tales told by his mother. One day, while Okonkwo and the boys are mending the compound wall, a swarm of locusts descends upon Umuofia. This rare event delights the villagers, since the locusts are good to eat.

While Okonkwo is eating locusts he is visited by one of the elders who tells him that the Oracle has decreed that Ikemefuna should be killed, as a sacrifice, but that, since the boy looks upon him as a father, Okonkwo should not take part in the killing. Pretending to be returning him to his home village, the men take Ikemefuna outside Umuofia and slay him, and, afraid of being thought weak, Okonkwo helps in the slaughter.

Nwoye is deeply affected by this incident which underlines the superstitious brutality of traditional Ibo society, a brutality that, with the coming of Christianity, is to be opposed by a religion preaching love and kindness.

NOTES AND GLOSSARY:
matchets: broad-bladed knives
ozo: the name of one of the Ibo titles or ranks

Chapter 8

Although Okonkwo is not a man of thought but of action, he has been very upset by the killing of Ikemefuna and is made sadder by the thought that his own son, Nwoye, is lacking in manliness. He visits his friend, Obierika, a man who takes a balanced view of things and who believes that Okonkwo should have played no part in the killing. Yet Okonkwo firmly believes that the commandments of the Oracle should be obeyed.

While he is in Obierika's hut, Okonkwo participates in the negotiations for the bride-price to be paid for the hand in marriage of Obierika's daughter, Akueke. She is a beautiful young girl of sixteen who is specially dressed in beads and body-paint for the occasion. A price of twenty bags of cowries is finally settled after lengthy and highly formal negotiations.

In this chapter we learn more of the customs and traditions of the tribe and gain insight into what the men talk about when they meet.

NOTES AND GLOSSARY:
plantains: a coarse type of banana used in cooking

bride-price:	the price paid by a suitor's family to the family of the girl he wants to marry
uli:	a dye used for body-painting
jigida:	a string of small beads hung round the waist of a girl or woman

Chapter 9

Ezinma, Okonkwo's daughter, who is his favourite child, catches malaria. Ekwefi, her mother, has had ten children but only Ezinma has survived infancy, and it is thought that, in her case, the evil spell cast upon Ekwefi's children had been broken through an elaborate magical ritual. Okonkwo gathers herbs and leaves from the bush and prepares an inhalation which cures Ezinma.

This chapter illustrates the magical beliefs and rituals of the tribe and shows how, before the coming of the white man, they had natural remedies and medicines for the commonest diseases. It is not accidental that a chapter dealing with malaria opens with an anecdote about the mosquito.

NOTES AND GLOSSARY:

diviner:	one who interprets the messages of the Oracle to the villagers
ogbanje:	a changeling; a child who repeatedly returns to its mother's womb to be reborn, yet always dies in infancy
iyi-uwa:	a special stone which links the *ogbanje* to the spirit-world, which, if it is discovered and destroyed, makes it possible for such a child to be kept alive

Chapter 10

In this chapter we see how justice is carried out in Umuofia. The case is one of a dispute between a husband and wife. The woman has returned to her family and her husband is now claiming back the bride-price from them. In reply, her family asserts that he has treated her harshly for nine years and that they are justified in taking her home.

The case is presented not just before the elders of the tribe but before the highest tribunal in the land, made up of the nine *egwugwu*, masked figures representing the ancestral spirits of each of the nine villages. Thus a magical as well as a legal force is lent to their judgement, which is one making for reconciliation between the disputing parties. It is clear that the second *egwugwu* is Okonkwo, but while he is masked he is not himself but one of the dead ancestors of the clan.

Chapter 11

It is a dark night and Ekwefi is telling her daughter, Ezinma, the legend of how the tortoise got its patterned shell, when Chielo, the priestess of the Oracle, arrives possessed by her spirit and claims that the Oracle wishes to see Ezinma. In spite of Ekwefi's protestations, she carries the child off into the night. Ekwefi follows the priestess and the child by a long, roundabout route to the cave, her love for her daughter overcoming her fear of the darkness. While, not daring to enter, she waits outside the cave, she discovers that Okonkwo too has followed. Thus not only is the couple's love for their daughter demonstrated, but also the way in which they are prepared to submit to the will of the gods.

NOTES AND GLOSSARY:
Tufia-a: a curse

Chapter 12

The following day is the day of the wedding-feast for Obierika's daughter. While Okonkwo's other wives and children go early to the feast, Okonkwo himself together with Ekwefi and Ezinma are delayed a little since they have been awake most of the night, and we learn of how the incident with the priestess ended and of Okonkwo's great concern for his daughter.

Preparations for the feast go ahead, with everyone taking part and contributing his share, and there are various incidents—a goat is slaughtered, a cow runs away—and informal gossip and conversation. When the suitor and his kinsfolk arrive, the formal ceremony begins. What happens is laid down by tradition, and it is noticeable that the occasion is a social (even a commercial) one, not a religious ceremony, involving feasting, singing and dancing and the telling of tales of past greatness.

NOTES AND GLOSSARY:
uri: marriage feast

Chapter 13

Ezeudu, the oldest man in Okonkwo's village, has died. He is the man who had warned Okonkwo to have no part in the slaughter of Ikemefuna. The whole land of Umuofia is in a turmoil of mourning: everyone laments and expresses his grief, and the *egwugwu*, visitors from the land of the ancestors to which Ezeudu is going, make frightening appearances.

As befits one of such high rank, the funeral ceremonies are very elaborate, being particularly marked by the firing of guns. At the height of the excitement there is a dreadful accident: Okonkwo's old gun explodes and the dead man's sixteen-year-old son is killed.

To kill a clansman is the greatest of crimes, and he who is responsible is banished from the land. However, since the killing was an accident, he is permitted to return after seven years. So Okonkwo and his family are forced before nightfall to flee to his distant native village of Mbanta, and when they are gone his compound and his possessions are destroyed by his fellow tribesmen in a ritual cleansing and purification of his sin.

NOTES AND GLOSSARY:

esoteric: secret, known only to a select few

age-groups: all men who have passed through the annual rituals of coming-of-age together are of the same age-group

---

Part Two, Chapter 14

Okonkwo has returned to Mbanta, his mother's home-village. He had last been there when he had taken his mother's body home for burial. His kinsfolk give him land for a compound and for cultivation and provide him with seed-yams, so Okonkwo plants again and tries to rebuild his fortune. But his heart is not in the task; he is in despair and feels that his personal god, his *chi*, is against him.

The final ceremonies completing the marriage of one of his cousins to a new wife take place and after the ceremony his uncle, Uchendu, takes Okonkwo to task for his despair. He has returned to the home of his mother, as a child runs to his mother for comfort when he is hurt, and it is displeasing to a mother when her child refuses to be comforted. So Okonkwo should not displease the spirit of his dead mother by despairing but should bend his efforts to providing for his wives and children during this period of exile.

NOTES AND GLOSSARY:

ochu: murder or manslaughter; a female *ochu* is a manslaughter that has been committed inadvertently

isa-ifi: a ceremony of confession which ensures that a wife has been faithful to her husband during a period of separation; also performed as the final ceremony of a marriage after the customary long period of betrothal

umuada: a gathering of all the female members of a family, usually on the occasion of a wedding or a funeral

Chapter 15

Two years have passed and Obierika has come to visit Okonkwo, bringing the money from the harvest of Okonkwo's yams. The visitors are greeted by Ochendu and the news they bring is of the first incursion of the white man into their land. One white man had arrived at the village of Abame, riding on a bicycle. Fearing that he would bring more of his kind, the villagers had killed him and, lest it should run away, had tied his machine to the sacred silk-cotton tree. Later, some other white men had come and, seeing the bicycle, had gone away again. One market-day the village had been secretly surrounded by many white men with guns who had massacred nearly all the inhabitants without warning. It is clear that Ibo society is going to come under increasing strain from the arrival of the white men, and, in discussion as to how to deal with the threat, it is Okonkwo's firm view that they should be met with violence.

NOTES AND GLOSSARY:
albino: one whose skin is abnormally white because it is devoid of pigment

Chapter 16

Another two years have passed and Obierika has again come to visit Okonkwo in exile. The missionaries have come to Umuofia and Obierika has discovered Okonkwo's son, Nwoye, among them, so he has come to discover how this has happened. Okonkwo will not tell him, but from Nwoye's mother he learns how one white missionary and his African evangelists had come to Mbanta. Most of the villagers, including Okonkwo, had scoffed at the preaching and the hymn-singing, but a few had been attracted by it. Amongst these was Nwoye, who had always felt unhappy at the violence and brutality of Ibo society, and who felt that the new religion offered hope of better things. He and his father are now estranged from one another.

Chapter 17

The missionaries had asked for land on which to build their church and the elders had granted them a plot in the 'Evil Forest', where no man goes and where those dying of infectious diseases, the magic belongings of dead witch-doctors, and other dangerous objects are left. It was hoped that this land would prove uninhabitable to the newcomers, but to everyone's surprise this 'bad medicine' did not seem to affect them. Even after seven market-weeks, which was thought to be the limit of the ancient spirits' tolerance, they were still there unharmed and gaining more converts.

Amongst these converts was Nwoye, who had hesitated a long time before joining them. When Okonkwo heard of this he had been very angry and had beaten his son. So Nwoye had left his father and gone to join the mission at Umuofia. Okonkwo feels that the fates have dealt him a sad blow in giving him such a son, so like his own dead father. He see his whole world crumbling about him and feels violent anger against the new faith. In Okonkwo's dilemma is forecast the destruction of traditional Ibo society.

NOTES AND GLOSSARY:

fetish: powerful objects in traditional magic; also the magic itself

Chapter 18

The gradually increasing strength of the mission is leading to violence between the two sides and it is rumoured that the white men are introducing government and laws to protect the missionaries. Preaching that all men are equal in the sight of God, the Christians admit to membership the outcasts of the tribe. This welcoming of prohibited castes, such as twins (who were always exposed by the Ibos to die in the forest), causes still more trouble with the villagers. When one of the converts deliberately kills a royal python, a most sacred creature in the eyes of the tribe, indignation boils over. Okonkwo is all for violent action, but the elders decide that the converts should be excluded from all the life and privileges of the tribe. However, the traditional gods show that they are still powerful when Okoli, who slew the python, falls ill and dies, and the villagers lift their ban.

NOTES AND GLOSSARY:

efulefu: idle good-for-nothings

osu: slaves, outcasts who, having been dedicated to a god, are not allowed to mix with the free-born

Chapter 19

Okonkwo's time of exile in Mbanta is drawing to a close. Although he has prospered there, he knows he would have done better in Umuofia and the thought makes him unhappy. Nevertheless, he gives a great feast to his kinsmen as a mark of his gratitude.

At this point in the novel this feast—a celebration of, and affirmation of, traditional values of kinship—forms an ironic counterpoint to the dangers that are threatening Ibo society, a gesture towards things as they were that are now beginning to fall apart.

NOTES AND GLOSSARY:

cassava: the West African name for manioc or tapioca, a root crop

umunna: a wide group of kinsmen

Part Three, Chapter 20

Okonkwo has returned to Umuofia. He has, of course, lost the opportunity of taking the highest titles and of leading his people in resistance to the new faith which has been spreading and gathering strength. Yet he resolves to re-establish his fortunes, to build a more splendid compound and to take two new wives. In spite of losing Nwoye, he still has five sons to be brought up in the traditional beliefs, and there is Ezinma, his favourite daughter, who has grown into a beautiful young woman and who he is determined will marry a worthy suitor from Umuofia.

But Umuofia has changed during his absence. A church has been established there, and also a court and a District Commissioner; offences against the white man's law are tried and men of rank in Ibo society imprisoned and put to unworthy labour under the supervision of African warders drawn from distant tribes. Okonkwo cannot understand why his people do not resist by force, but Obierika, who knows the practical realities, points out that resistance is useless since their society is being undermined from inside and many of their fellow-tribesmen now disapprove of the old ways. Even when the new law seems unjust by the old standards it will have to be accepted.

NOTES AND GLOSSARY:

kotma: court messengers

Chapter 21

The coming of the white man has, in fact, brought increasing prosperity to Umuofia. The position of the mission is strengthened by the missionary, Mr Brown, who tries to learn something of the traditional ways and keeps his converts from excesses of zeal. Though Mr Brown does not succeed in converting one of the prominent citizens called Akunna to the idea that there is but One God, Akunna does send one of his sons to be taught in the mission-school. And in learning something of the nature of the old religion, Mr Brown realises that it is only in indirect ways, by building a school and a hospital, that he can hope to overcome. In this way his influence spreads rapidly.

Nwoye had been baptised a Christian under the name of Isaac and had left for a teacher-training college. This is a cause of great sorrow to Okonkwo whose triumphant return to Umuofia has been quite spoilt. He finds Umuofia a different land, with new interests, no longer a land of warriors.

NOTES AND GLOSSARY:

Ikenga: personal or household god, carved as an idol

Chapter 22

Mr Brown, who has become ill and left the mission, is replaced by Mr Smith, a narrow-minded and very rigid Christian who makes no effort to understand Ibo ways and refuses to compromise with them. Thus the more zealous converts flourish. One of them is Enoch who, it is believed, killed and ate the sacred python. It is this man who touches off the great conflict between the converts and the clansmen by committing the unheard-of crime of unmasking an *egwugwu* during the ceremonies to the earth-goddess. This arouses the elders of the tribe who, after a great gathering, destroy Enoch's compound, and then, after a confrontation between the traditional forces and the representative of the new faith, Mr Smith, they burn the church to the ground. If Mr Smith is prepared to learn and understand their ways, then he is free to live among them and practise his religion.

NOTES AND GLOSSARY:

Baal: a false god, originally a god of the Phoenicians
ogwu: magic

Chapter 23

Okonkwo is very pleased that at last the tribe has acted. He, along with another five leaders of the clan, is invited to the court-house to discuss the matter with the District Commissioner. There, by a trick, they are arrested and handcuffed. They are charged and fined for molesting others and destroying property. While they are in detention waiting for the fine to be collected from their people, they are maltreated by the court messengers and their heads shaved. The village is stunned and powerless before the white man's law and agrees to pay the fine.

Chapter 24

The men return in silence to the village, Okonkwo nursing in his heart a bitter hatred of the white man for the humiliation he has suffered, and swearing to be revenged and to fight alone if need be. A great meeting of the tribesmen is called, and while they are deciding that they have been pushed to the limit and that they will have to fight, even if it means attacking their kinsmen, the court messengers appear with orders to stop the meeting. Trembling with hatred and not stopping to think, Okonkwo draws his matchet and strikes the head messenger dead. Since the other messengers have been allowed to escape, he knows that his people will not fight.

Chapter 25

The District Commissioner and his soldiers arrive at Okonkwo's compound to find Obierika and others of his friends sitting there. They offer to take the Commissioner and his men to where Okonkwo is, if they will help them. They take them into the bush to where Okonkwo has hanged himself from a tree. Since suicide is an abomination, an offence against the gods, it is not permitted for his fellow-tribesmen to cut him down and bury him, or even to touch him. The Commissioner does not understand the people or the customs but nevertheless plans to include the incident in a paragraph of a book he is writing.

It is left to Obierika to speak Okonkwo's epitaph: 'That man was one of the greatest men in Umuofia. You drove him to kill himself; and now he will be buried like a dog.'

Part 3

Commentary

ALL NOVELS are imaginative, artificial constructions which represent some aspect of real life, either in the present or the past. They cannot, of course, be *total* representations, for the novelist must select from real life those features that best transmit or illustrate his story. In a sense, he is creating a little world that is merely a portion of the real world and how he sees it. The reason he does this is, of course, to tell his story in the way that most moves us, or impresses us; but the reason he tells the story at all is in order to explain to us what happened, how it happened, why it happened and, in the most general terms, to explain to us that section of real life that he has chosen to present.

Since it is created or constructed, it follows, therefore, that a novel can be considered from several aspects; that the various parts that go to make it up can be considered separately, since they must have been considered separately by the novelist in creating his work. Of course, since a novel is (or ought to be) a unified whole, these parts can never be entirely separated—for example, the characters of those in the novel may produce the action while at the same time the events may act upon the characters—but it is most convenient, and often revealing, to consider these different aspects of the novel separately. In this respect, *Things Fall Apart* is no different from any other novel.

The main aspects of a novel that have to be considered by the student or by anyone wishing to enrich their understanding of the work are:

The tale: what happens in the novel; sometimes called the 'story';
Plot and structure: the plan of the tale and the order in which it is presented;
The characters;
Theme(s): what the novel is about, including the author's purpose in writing it;
Language and style: how the tale is told.

The tale

In Part 2 you will find summaries of *Things Fall Apart*—first of all a general summary and then summaries of each chapter taken in turn. Though these summaries include the tale or story, they also include much more—the plot, the circumstances, the characters and so on. A summary of the story alone, of what happens in the novel, can be much barer and much shorter and it should be possible to make such a summary in a very few sentences.

Indeed, it is worth making such a summary of every novel you read. You will notice that very often reviews of novels include just such a summary in order that prospective readers of the book will have some idea of whether it will interest them or not. Sometimes, too, a summary of the story is printed on the back of a book or on the fly-leaf for the same purpose; and this may be an extract from a review of the book that has appeared in a newspaper.

For example, on the back of the current edition of *Things Fall Apart* is printed a brief extract from a review of the novel written by Angus Wilson in *The Observer*, a leading London weekly newspaper:

> The story is the tragedy of Okonkwo, an important man in the Ibo tribe in the days when white men were first appearing on the scene. . . . Mr Achebe's very simple but excellent novel tells of the series of events by which Okonkwo through his pride and his fears becomes exiled from his tribe and returns only to be forced into the ignominy of suicide to escape the results of his rash courage against the white man.

This is, in some seventy-five words, a masterly summary of the book—as might be expected from Mr Wilson, himself a leading contemporary novelist—yet even a passage as short as this contains much that is additional to a mere summary of the story.

For a start, Mr Wilson's summary includes criticism ('Mr Achebe's very simple but excellent novel . . .'), and it includes something of his interpretation or understanding of the novel. Is it true, for example, that Okonkwo is exiled 'through his pride and his fears'? And do you think it is correct to say that Okonkwo commits suicide 'to escape the results of his rash courage against the white man'? At least, those questions are open to debate.

The fact of the matter is that each person will make a slightly different summary of the story and place his own interpretation upon it, since it is impossible to disentangle the various parts of the novel entirely. What happens in the novel is not merely a matter of accidental incident and event, but is often produced by the nature of the characters in the story. Thus, while the exploding of Okonkwo's gun is a purely accidental event (though prepared for in that we have previously learnt that the gun is old and rusty), the killing of Ikemefuna by Okonkwo comes about because Okonkwo's pride has insisted on his being present. Nevertheless, writing a summary of the tale is always a useful exercise. It clarifies your thinking and often brings the other parts of the novel into sharp focus.

Here is one attempt at such a summary (yours will be different):

> The novel tells the tragic story of Okonkwo, who cannot adjust to the changes brought about in his tribe by the arrival of the white man and the disruption of the life he knows and approves. Failing to rouse his fellows against the interlopers, he takes violent action, but, seeing there is no hope for the old order, commits suicide.

And here is another summary:

> This novel tells of the effect of the arrival of the white man and his ideas upon the life of a hitherto secluded West African tribe and of how one man attempts to resist change, and, finally despairing, takes his own life.

Do you think either of these summaries is correct? If so, which? Or do you think neither is correct—or both? Already, you will see, you have focused your mind more closely upon some of the features of the book and whether it is more a story about Okonkwo and his character or more a story about effects of change upon a simple people. These are matters to consider separately later, but already you are beginning to see that the two matters are interwoven.

At its least, of course, what *happens* in a story is a mere matter of re-counting the incidents or events in chronological order. Indeed, there are some stories—such as thrillers—which are little more than a succession of events and the characters are mere lifeless puppets to whom things happen. But in most stories of value the events are happening to people we have grown to care about, or are in some way produced by the natures or decisions of those characters, and the events are mostly of interest for the way in which they affect the characters. Thus the events, by themselves, are not the whole story.

Many students, when asked a question about a novel or asked to comment upon it, content themselves with re-telling—often in great detail—the story or a portion of it. This is never what is wanted. It is sufficient to refer to the incidents or the story, giving brief examples and, where appropriate, quotations. What is wanted is *your* comment upon, or interpretation of, the story or the events. Simple narrative is not enough.

Naturally the tale—what happens in the novel, the events and incidents of the story—matters. Its main importance, however, is as a framework into which all the other bits are fitted. The way in which this framework is shaped is known as the 'plot'.

Plot and structure

The plot is the plan of the story and particularly concerns the order in which the events are presented to the reader; that is to say, it is particularly concerned with time. A story might have a very simple plot and recount the events as they happened in the strict order in which they happened. Or its time-sequence might be very complicated—operating, for example, by 'flashback', or holding back certain of the events until later in the interest of creating suspense, or anticipating an event by some earlier glimpse of it. Even the simplest tale, told in apparently chronological order, may use some of these devices.

However, any plot or plan has a shape. Some bits are merely sketched in or suggested; others are left out altogether for us to assume; still others are of an importance that means that they are dealt with in much more detail or much more extensively. In other words, the plot is so arranged as to give us a structure. It is common, for example, for the complications of a story to rise slowly to a crisis or climax (usually towards the end) which is unravelled in the final pages, but it is probably preceded by a number of minor climaxes, each with its part to play in arousing and maintaining our interest and in building towards the major climax. The structure has a lot to do with the feeling of satisfying wholeness that we have when we finish reading a good novel. A story which rambles on without an adequate plot and which is inadequately proportioned or structured is a very boring story indeed.

Things Fall Apart is plotted in the simplest way. It starts with Okonkwo: 'Okonkwo was well known throughout the nine villages and even beyond.' Then it follows the events of his lifetime and ends with his death and the Commissioner's decision to devote a paragraph to it in the book he is contemplating writing. Even the main events which take place at which Okonkwo is not present—such as the murder of the missionary and the massacre of Abam—are told as they are reported to him and thus are seen, in a sense, from his point of view.

At first glance the plot simply follows the events of Okonkwo's life one by one from his adult years. In general, each chapter gives an event or an episode in the story, and so the plotting is of the kind we call 'episodic'. Yet a glance at the first few chapters will show us that the events do not just follow one another in chronological order like beads upon a string.

Chapter 1 introduces us to Okonkwo at about the age of forty. Yet almost immediately it moves to telling us about how 'twenty years or more' ago he had defeated Amalinze the Cat in wrestling, and three-quarters of the chapter concerns Okonkwo's father, who had died ten years ago, and over half of this short biography of Unoka is illuminated by a detailed account of the interview with Okoye to whom he owes money. All this is long in the past and does not directly concern Okon-kwo; yet in the last paragraph we are returned to Okonkwo and the present, while at the very end we are cast forward both to an event that is not recounted until Chapter 2 (Okonkwo's acquiring guardianship of the hostage) and, in the phrases 'doomed lad' and 'ill-fated lad' that are used of Ikemefuna, to the slaughter of the boy, which is an event that does not take place until Chapter 7, three years later.

In Chapter 2 we learn how Ikemefuna came into Okonkwo's house-hold; yet even this account is interrupted by a page in which we learn how Okonkwo rules his household. Then in Chapter 3 we move right back in time to learn more of Unoka and of how Okonkwo got his start in life. Only with Chapter 4 does the story begin to move forward in time again. In that chapter and in Chapters 5 and 6 the story is proceed-ing in an episodic way with the Week of Peace, the planting of the yams, the harvesting with the Feast of the New Yam and the wrestling contest. And in Chapter 7, introduced by the episode of the locusts, we come to the first major incident of the novel, the god-ordained slaughter of Ikemefuna.

An examination of the rest of the novel will show that the same pro-cess of arranging the order in which events are presented to the reader is going on throughout. The purpose of this is to present the events in a way which gives the story most force and power, conveying the events in a succession and with the degree of emphasis that create the most impression upon the reader, arousing and sustaining his interest and best transmitting the novelist's desired atmosphere and chosen themes.

We have been following closely Achebe's plotting in a small section of the novel. But the novel has a larger-scale plan which we can see best by standing a little way back from the work.

The novel is divided into three unequal parts, Part One being longer than the other two parts put together. Little of what we would put into a brief one-sentence summary of the story appears in these thirteen chapters yet they form over half the book.

The reason that Achebe devotes so much time and space to this part of the novel is that one of his main themes is that of change, coming to an established society. Thus he has to make the form and nature of that society plain to us by demonstrating the sort of activities in which it engages, the sort of beliefs it has and the way in which it is organised. After all, the sort of tribal society he is re-creating is one which will be foreign and strange to most of his readers. It will even be strange to most of his West African readers, since what he is showing is a way of life that has passed from living memory.

He could, of course, have done the same by writing a sociological account or a historical treatise. That would not have been nearly so effective as the work of fiction he has chosen, for a novel is about human beings and their reaction to circumstances—human beings whom we grow to know and with whom we become involved. *Things Fall Apart* is specifically about Okonkwo in this society, and about his family and friends and acquaintances. So in Chapter 10, for example, where we get the judging by the *egwugwu* of a marriage-dispute, we are transported by the magic of the writer's art to be actually present on that occasion, since we know and are involved with the people who are participating. This we could never have got from a dry, sociological account together with a scientific commentary. We seem to be actually there, almost as if we ourselves were participating.

The true climax of Part One comes almost casually in the last chapter when, at Ezeudu's funeral, Okonkwo's gun explodes and kills the youth. This disaster is what sets in train the rest of the story, bringing about Okonkwo's exile and, ultimately, his downfall.

But before this there have been a number of minor incidents in episodes which serve either to illuminate the tribal society or to illuminate significantly Okonkwo's character. In the first category we have episodes such as the celebratory wrestling-contest in Chapter 6, the *egwugwu* judgement of Chapter 10 and the marriage arrangements and feast of Chapters 8 and 12. More significant for the story are episodes of the second sort which reveal something of importance about Okonkwo's character. Such are Chapter 9 in which Ezinma is cured of malaria and Chapter 11 in which she is carried off by the priestess. Both of these show the gentler and more kindly side of Okonkwo's outwardly stern and unbending nature.

Undoubtedly, however, the one important minor climax in Part One occurs in Chapter 7 with the murder of Ikemefuna. It builds up to a split-second moment where Okonkwo resolves the conflict between his love for the boy and his fear of being thought weak for failing to carry out the orders of the gods:

> As the man who had cleared his throat drew up and raised his matchet, Okonkwo looked away. He heard the blow. The pot fell and broke in the sand. He heard Ikemefuna cry, 'My father, they have killed me!' as he ran towards him. Dazed with fear, Okonkwo drew his matchet and cut him down. He was afraid of being thought weak.

This chapter, which produces the climax in the middle of Part One, repays very close examination. It is one of the most touching and moving incidents in the novel. Like Okonkwo, we have grown very fond of Ikemefuna, and the chapter has opened with Okonkwo and the two boys engaged in happy activity about the compound. Then we learn, with as much shock and surprise as Okonkwo does, what is to be his fate. Deceived into thinking he is being taken home, Ikemefuna is walked out into the bush. At this point we are taken into his mind and made party to his thoughts—something unusual in a novel in which it is normally Okonkwo's thoughts we hear. He thinks of his home and of his mother and sister. He even sings to himself a child's counting-out song. All the time we know that it is he who is to be 'counted out', and we view his thoughts in the light of this knowledge. The effect is extraordinarily sad, even tragic, and it underlines the senseless brutality of a society in which such things can happen by the command of an inhumane god—as the sensitive Nwoye immediately realises. Okonkwo's action, too, sudden and unpremeditated, echoes his rashness in firing his gun at his wife (Chapter 5) and foreshadows the violent action of the end of the novel.

Part Two of the novel could easily be entitled *Exile*, since it starts with Okonkwo's arrival in Mbanta and ends with the feast he gives his kinsmen as he prepares to return to Umuofia. It is during this period that the first impact of the arrival of the white man is felt by the forest tribes and it is significant that much of what is happening in Umuofia is reported to Okonkwo by Obierika. This underlines Okonkwo's impotence, his inability to take any action—something he has always found frustrating and irritating—and the build-up of tension and anger within him is increased, leading to the violent action at the end of Part Three.

The seven years of Okonkwo's exile are covered in only six chapters, and the story has begun to take very big steps in time. Chapter 15 takes place two years after Chapter 14, and Chapter 16 is another two years later, with Chapters 18 and 19 covering the last three years of exile. Yet there is movement even within this time-scale, since, for example, in Chapter 15 Obierika is reporting incidents that have happened previously and in Chapter 17 we move back slightly to discover how the missionaries came to Mbanta and how Nwoye was converted.

The climax of Part Two does not reside in a single violent incident that reaches its peak in action described in a few brief sentences. It resides rather in the whole of Chapter 19 in which Okonkwo gives a great feast of thanks to his mother's kinsfolk. We are reminded here of Achebe's great-grandfather, Udo Osinyi, who was renowned for his open-handed generosity in the size and scale of the feasts he put on for his relatives. It is the sort of feast that took place, and could only take place, in the traditional Ibo social context. We are aware, of course, that this traditional order of things is under threat. This is the whole message of Part Two, and in this position in the novel the feast constitutes a defiant assertion and affirmation of all the traditional ways of doing things and all the traditional values. As the oldest member of the family says in his speech:

It is good in these days when the younger generation consider themselves wiser than their sires to see a man doing things in the grand, old

way. . . . I fear for the younger generation, for you people. . . . I fear
for you young people because you do not understand how strong is
the bond of kinship. You do not know what it is to speak with one
voice. And what is the result? An abominable religion has settled
among you. A man can now leave his father and his brothers. He can
curse the gods of his fathers and his ancestors, like a hunter's dog that
suddenly goes mad and turns on his master. I fear for you; I fear for
the clan.

Part Three, which is exactly the same length as Part Two, seems to move
much more swiftly. This is because it is made up largely of action which
is closely linked, in that one incident leads naturally to the next in a
chain of cause and effect.

On Okonkwo's return, Umuofia has changed and the white man's
law has been established. Everything goes fairly smoothly under the
first missionary, who is sensitive to the nature of the Ibo people and to
the fact that their social order is not lightly to be disrupted. But with the
arrival of a new missionary the scene is set for trouble. The murder of
the sacred python brings about the destruction of the mission-church
(Chapter 22). This, in turn, brings about the arrest and humiliation of
Okonkwo and the elders (Chapter 23). From this comes the protest-
meeting and the murder of the messenger (Chapter 24) and thus Okonkwo's tragic end. The incidents are naturally—and inevitably—inter-
connected and, closely associated in time as they are, sweep us on with
increasing pace to the climax at the public meeting where, once again,
Okonkwo acts suddenly and without care of the consequences.

Yet even here the tragic movement is not completed. The novel is the
story of Okonkwo and there must be consequences for him in his actions
—his tale has to be rounded off.

At first, in the final chapter, we are deliberately kept from knowing
what has happened; and, indeed, we are kept from Okonkwo in his final
hour. This, it should be noted, is the common practice in the ancient
Greek tragic drama, where we are never allowed to be present at the
death of the hero. One result of this is to create in us the feeling that, in
the act of dying, the hero is already moving away from the world of men
into the otherworld of death. So it is with Okonkwo. He dies alone and
in a way that Ibo tradition considers most shameful, and in ironic contrast to the fame and nobility which we saw him enjoying in the first
chapter of the novel.

It is his old friend, Obierika, who speaks his obituary and his condemnation of the new regime, and in so doing sums up the whole story:

That man was one of the greatest men in Umuofia. You drove him to
kill himself; and now he will be buried like a dog. . . .

Thus the ends of the story are tied together and it attains completeness.

But there is a final ironic twist which comments upon the whole story and sets it in its wider context of African colonialism. The Commissioner thinks about putting the incident in the book he is writing:

> One could almost write a whole chapter on him. Perhaps not a whole chapter but a reasonable paragraph, at any rate. There was so much else to include, and one must be firm in cutting out details. He had already chosen the title of the book, after much thought: *The Pacification of the Primitive Tribes of the Lower Niger*.

Suddenly the whole story of Okonkwo and his people in which we have been so engrossed for so many hundreds of paragraphs is strangely diminished. It is as if we were looking down the wrong end of a telescope. But, of course, the effect of this is merely to remind us that Okonkwo's tragedy is not something petty and insignificant at all, that the Commissioner is wrong, that the wide view of history that ignores the individual circumstances of human beings is wrong. And the title of the Commissioner's projected book is, in the light of *Things Fall Apart*, packed with ironies.

There are lesser actions going on through the novel which contribute to its total effect in an accumulating and not a carefully plotted way. In this manner we acquire a knowledge of all the customs of the tribe—its festivals and celebrations, tied to the seasons and to sowing and harvest-time, its religious rituals, its way of administering justice. We are even given, at appropriate points and in order, the various stages of the celebration of marriage, with the arranging of the bride-price in Chapter 8, the feast at the bride's household in Chapter 12 and (though this is another marriage) the final ceremony in the husband's household in Chapter 14. Similarly, we gradually build up a picture of social customs and of how life is actually lived in Okonkwo's compound.

Okonkwo's views and attitudes are slowly built up in the discussions and debates which take place in almost every chapter, particularly in the series of discussions with his friend Obierika that run through Parts Two and Three, in the discussions with others and in the public debates, culminating in the fatal debate in Chapter 24 where Okonkwo finally senses that his people will do nothing to resist the intruders.

Things Fall Apart is, after all, only partly a matter of incidents and events presented to us in a certain order. It is a story of human beings, in particular of Okonkwo, and it is in the individually created characters of these human beings that more than half the story lies.

The characters

Novels are not merely accounts of events. They are accounts of events happening to *people*; and these are people whom we get to know intimately, and feel for. We read novels only because we are interested in these human beings and how they react to the circumstances in which they find themselves or create for themselves, and we can get to know the characters in fiction better than we get to know any real persons other than ourselves. Indeed, it is an ironic fact that many of the characters in fiction (in novels, say, or drama), who have never had any real existence other than in the mind of their creator, are more 'real' to us than people who have actually existed. For example, we know Shakespeare's Falstaff, who never lived, much better than we know Elizabeth I of England, who did, such is the intense reality in our imaginations of the shadowy creation of a writer's mind. This is why the study of fictional creations such as plays or novels matters. It is the only study which concerns itself solely with man—in relation to himself, to his fellow-men and to his God and the cosmos. It follows, therefore, that we must pay close attention to the characters in the novels we study.

In real life we get to know other human beings in two main ways—we know what they look like and we know what they say and do. We do not have to make very much effort over their appearance, since they are there before our eyes, but we make a great many deductions about them from their behaviour. Whether or not we are correct in these deductions does not matter. We keep changing them as we get to know the characters better and what we end up with is our own appraisal of them.

The novelist's problem is that he has to make his imagined characters 'real' to us. Thus, since the character is not before our eyes, he must, as a rule, spend some time in describing his appearance. What sort of character he is has to be revealed by the novelist gradually through his story. The novelist is actually *creating* the character and it would be a mistake to think of him as doing this haphazardly or other than by an act of deliberate and careful consideration. Since he is creating his little world and all that is in it, rather like a god, he has one great privilege and aid in his task. He knows everything and can if he wishes (and he often does) comment upon his characters and explain their actions. In addition, he can take us right inside the minds of his characters so that they can show or explain their thoughts and motives to us—something that can never happen in real life.

While there are, of course, novels in which the plotting of the incidents is dominant and the characters purely incidental to the exciting events, in any serious novel in which there is a genuine attempt to re-create real life or a passable imitation of it, the imagined characters are all-important. If we imagine the novel as a piece of woven tapestry with a warp and a weft, then the plot is the warp and the characters are the weft. The one is interwoven with the other and the more densely the two are packed the richer and more elaborate is the final effect.

There can be few novels that produce a final effect that is more rich and strange from such an economical use of materials than *Things Fall Apart*. And, as we are discovering, there can be few that have been more carefully planned and precisely executed. Not the least of Achebe's feats in this novel is the success with which he has brought alive to us the tribesmen of a distant time, living in circumstances that are very remote and foreign to most of us, and has made them into living and breathing human beings with whom we can identify, with whose hopes and fears we can sympathise and with whose minds we can enter into an understanding, in our common humanity. This is the miracle which a fiction writer can perform. It is the miracle Achebe performs in creating his characters.

Okonkwo

The principal character of *Things Fall Apart* is Okonkwo. Some people would call him the 'hero' of the book. 'Hero' may be a very little word, but it is one that is full of meaning. Traditionally, it is applied to a man of great nobility and courage, who fights bravely and whose feats have become almost legendary amongst his people. It is not the sort of word that should, properly, be applied to the principal character of just any story—though it often is. However, it is, indeed, properly applied to Okonkwo, since his society is one that sets very great store by such feats of personal courage and such personal qualities as he displays. Modern society, with its complexity and its stress upon qualities of gentleness and humanity, does not easily produce such men.

Of course, a character who displays nothing but good qualities of one sort would be rather flat and uninteresting, and Achebe does not fall into this mistake. According to one ancient view of the hero, he is a noble man whose tragic end is brought about by some flaw in his character, who, in a sense, produces his own tragedy since the seeds of it are always there inside him. Achebe does not make Okonkwo all good and all noble, without any flaws, but he takes pains to make him fully rounded and believable, a real human being with doubts and fears and questionings as well as the simpler and more straightforward virtues. Achebe takes care to give us his appearance on the very first page:

> He was tall and huge, and his bushy eyebrows and wide nose gave him a very severe look. He breathed heavily, and it was said that, when he slept, his wives and children in their out-houses could hear him breathe. When he walked, his heels hardly touched the ground and he seemed to walk on springs, as if he was going to pounce on somebody. And he did pounce on people quite often. He had a slight stammer and whenever he was angry and could not get his words out quickly enough, he would use his fists. He had no patience with un-successful men.

This is very much the sort of man we would expect one who had been such a famous wrestler to be, and it is clearly the sort of man that the Ibos—who are not the tallest of men—would admire. Later on, among the *egwugwu* in Chapter 10, it is by his walk that we can recognise Okonkwo under his disgûise:

> Okonkwo's wives, and perhaps other women as well, might have noticed that the second *egwugwu* had the springy walk of Okonkwo.

All in all, the description of Okonkwo, both here and wherever else it is mentioned, is one that fits a man of his character and reputation— active, strong and physically energetic. So we are not surprised to find him described in Chapter 2 as:

> a man of action, a man of war. . . . In Umuofia's latest war he was the first to bring home a human head. That was his fifth head; and he was not an old man yet.

In addition to success in war and fighting, Okonkwo has been very successful in other ways:

> He was a wealthy farmer and had two barns full of yams, and had just married his third wife. To crown it all he had taken two titles and had shown incredible prowess in two inter-tribal wars. And so although Okonkwo was still young, he was already one of the greatest men of his time.

In Chapter 3 we learn by what prodigious efforts of industry and hard work, struggling against difficult odds, he had attained this position. As it is summed up at the beginning of Chapter 4:

> it was really not true that Okonkwo's palm-kernels had been cracked for him by a benevolent spirit. He had cracked them himself. Anyone who knew his grim struggle against poverty and misfortune could not say he had been lucky. If ever a man deserved his success, that man was Okonkwo.

That is a very straightforward summing-up, such as we ourselves might make, but then Achebe goes on to put this discussion in the terms that an Ibo might use:

> At the most one could say that his *chi* or personal god was good. But the Ibo people have a proverb that when a man says yes his *chi* says yes also. Okonkwo said yes very strongly; so his *chi* agreed. And not only his *chi* but his clan too, because it judged a man by the work of his hands.

This passage exemplifies the basic Ibo view of the universe. There is the everyday world of here and now and there is the otherworld of the spirit. The two run parallel to one another and intermingle one with the other. Okonkwo's *chi* is his equivalent in the spirit world, affecting him and being affected by him. He is a man of such positive power that his *chi*—which has something of the qualities of a personal god or good angel and something also of the qualities of fate—has to go along with him.

Very early in the novel, however, we learn what is Okonkwo's motivation or driving force. It is fear—fear of being regarded as a weak man and a failure in society as his father, Unoka, was. That is why Achebe devotes so much time in the first three chapters to the life and character of Okonkwo's father. He brings out the reason for Okonkwo's exaggerated idea of manliness by establishing Unoka as a character of an almost opposite type—gentle, interested in the softer and more kindly aspects of life, improvident, idle and unsuccessful. Achebe does not condemn Unoka but makes it clear why Okonkwo is ashamed of him. Thus we learn, in Chapter 2:

> And so Okonkwo was ruled by one passion—to hate everything that his father Unoka had loved. One of those things was gentleness and another was idleness.

As we might expect, such a man is stern and harsh, even in his dealings with his own family, since 'to show affection was a sign of weakness'. He loves action and scorns inactivity, perhaps because it would give him too much time for thought; and, with a very clear idea of what, from the traditional Ibo point of view, is correct and proper, is inclined to act precipitately and without thought.

Such a character, strongly established by Achebe, is perhaps too positive to be entirely credible. And so Okonkwo is shown as having a gentler side, fully capable of human emotions and affections. This is first shown in the fact that he becomes fond of Ikemefuna and is distressed and upset for several days after his murder, but it is shown still more in his attitude towards his daughter, Ezinma, and her mother, Ekwefi. Ekwefi is the only one of his three wives whose name we learn; she is constantly involved in the story; and in Chapter 9 with his concern over Ezinma's malaria and in Chapter 11 where he overcomes his fear of the supernatural and follows the priestess we get a clear view of the depth of Okonkwo's love for his daughter. During his exile (Chapter 20) he influences Ezinma to marry only a man from Umuofia, so that, through his daughter, he will still retain prestige in his clan. She is everything his son, Nwoye, is not, and their relationship is very close. Had Nwoye conformed more to his ideal of manliness, had he been more a carbon-copy of himself and less like the father of whom he is ashamed, we can be sure that Okonkwo would have loved him too. As it is, he disowns Nwoye (Chapter 17) for what he sees to be the enormity of his crime:

> To abandon the gods of one's father and go about with a lot of effeminate men clucking like old hens was the very depth of abomination. Suppose when he died all his male children decided to follow Nwoye's steps and abandon their ancestors? Okonkwo felt a cold shudder run through him at the terrible prospect, like the prospect of annihilation. He saw himself and his father crowding round their ancestral shrine waiting in vain for worship and sacrifice and finding nothing but ashes of bygone days, and his children the while praying to the white man's god. If such a thing were ever to happen, he, Okonkwo, would wipe them off the face of the earth.

This is the man who is nicknamed 'Roaring Flame', whose temper flares up as suddenly as a tropical storm, the man who is so violent that he threatens his remaining five sons that, if they turn against him, 'when I am dead I will visit you and break your neck' (Chapter 20).

By showing the various, and sometimes contradictory, aspects of Okonkwo's nature, Achebe has created a fully rounded character. If he often acts rashly and impetuously, he just as often has second thoughts after the event. When he breaks the Week of Peace in Chapter 4, 'Inwardly he was repentant. But he was not the man to go about telling his neighbours that he was in error.' He is too proud to admit that he is mistaken, which his clansmen see as a defect in his character. Similarly, when he has recovered from his period of moping after the death of Ikemefuna, he does not say a word to his family or his friend, Obierika, about his sorrow. But we, the readers, have been privileged to know his thoughts and we know that, inside, his feelings have been at war with his sense of duty. Always his sense of duty, duty to the traditions of his ancestors, prevails.

Throughout the story as it develops, we are made to know Okonkwo's thoughts. This lets us know that he is not quite the simple, one-point-of-view man that we might imagine if we only saw his actions and heard what he said out loud. Thus we are able to follow his reactions to outside events and the changes that are taking place in the fabric of Ibo life, and come into sympathy with him. While we might not entirely approve of his point of view, at least we are enabled to understand it and to feel for him in the dilemmas in which he is placed. He becomes a character we really know and understand, for whom we develop an affection and liking, whose faults we are prepared to overlook, since we can see clearly how they came about.

The Okonkwo of Part One is Okonkwo at the height of his powers. With his exile he loses his place in the clan and, while he is happy enough in Mbanta, some of the heart has gone out of him. He is beginning to face increasing odds, and part of the fascination of the rest of the story lies in watching the indomitable courage with which he faces up to a fate that is against him. We can guess the outcome, since we know that the old cannot for ever stand out against the new.

Yet this outcome turns out to be worse than we had imagined possible. His fear of being thought 'unmanly' has a weakness in it that is clearly recognised by his fellows during his period of prosperity. His apparent pride is not a very attractive feature of his character, and only Achebe's readers are allowed to know that this springs from his fear of being thought weak. When this fear is uppermost he acts rashly, like one possessed: in killing Ikemefuna he is 'dazed with fear'. Increasingly as the story progresses, Okonkwo's fear, which is something in his mind, is supplanted by the reality of the destruction of the manly and warrior-like qualities of his people. The things that have happened to the people of Umuofia, their impotence in the face of the power of the white man and, in particular, the humiliation in captivity of Okonkwo and the elders, at last convince him that his clansmen have 'unaccountably become soft like women' (Chapter 21). With the burning of the church he becomes, briefly, almost happy again, but when after the humiliation he is set free (Chapter 24) he swears vengeance: 'If Umuofia decided on war, all would be well. But if they chose to be cowards he would go out and avenge himself.' This, in fact, is what happens. He knows in his heart that the people of Umuofia will not fight, and this is confirmed when, after he slays the head messenger, they allow the other messengers to escape. The people are frightened, not angry, and he knows that the fabric of his world, the world into which he was born and whose traditions he has always upheld, has crumbled.

Although we are not with him at his end, we now know Okonkwo's character well enough to hazard a guess at what is in his mind. The world he knew has gone: the world that is coming has no place for one of his uncompromising nature. He cannot, singlehanded, take on the new powers that have destroyed the old. So he opts to join his ancestors, the men of the old order, the warriors he reveres. He chooses to commit suicide, the most shameful way to die, abominated by gods and men alike. The things that he has known have fallen apart and have dragged him down with them.

We are now in a position to draw up a list of the attributes of Okonkwo's character. On the good side, he is strong, brave, hardworking, energetic and loves action. He has within himself a capacity for love. But on the bad side, he is unbending and inflexible, unwilling to show the more kindly part of his nature, and is given to rash and impetuous action, without thought. Yet, since we know him 'from the inside' as it were, we understand and are prepared to forgive his faults and to mourn over his inevitable tragedy. His faults are the faults of his virtues—a loyal and unquestioning obedience to the old, the traditional, Ibo way of life.

Unoka

Unoka is the opposite of Okonkwo. He is weak, idle, improvident and not in any way manly. The traditional Ibo society has little regard for such a man, and, of course, his very existence is the reason for much of the nature of Okonkwo, who tries, as much as possible, to be unlike his father.

However, Achebe does not in any way condemn Unoka. The things Unoka likes, such as flute-playing and music, are important aspects of Ibo life, and one feels that Achebe has, as one might expect, a great deal of sympathy for Unoka's tastes, for the poet as opposed to the man of action. Even Okonkwo has respect for such abilities, and in Chapter 24 praises Okudo, who was not a warrior but 'who sang a war song in a way that no other man could'. We cannot, however, imagine that he would think equally highly of a man who sang love songs!

Though Unoka is in the novel as a contrast to Okonkwo, it is undoubted that, without Unoka, we should miss a whole area of Ibo life and think the Ibos to be a fierce and warlike people, with no interest in the arts and the finer side of life—not at all the nation that could produce an Achebe.

Nwoye

Since Unoka dies near the beginning of the novel, part of his function in expressing the gentler and more artistic side of Ibo life passes to Nwoye, who is frequently likened to his grandfather. But Nwoye is living in different times, and part of our interest in him lies in observing how one of his nature responds to the new ideas. Okonkwo despises him, of course, but younger readers will well be able to feel for him in having such a father.

Nwoye is extremely sensitive and with him feelings come first, then thought, and a long way after, action. He it is who loves legends and folk-tales. He it is who first senses that Ikemefuna has been killed, and the way in which he links this with the practice of exposing twins to die in the forest shows that, long before the coming of the white man, he is already questioning the barbarity of some of the old customs. Since he is afraid of his father, he hesitates at first to join the Christians, but it is his father's violence and opposition that finally drive him away to attend the mission-school in Umuofia. He sees in the new faith some sort of answer to the problems that have troubled him about the old and we see in his survival, echoing the interests of his grandfather,

Achebe's affirmation of the continuity of these particular values.

Unoka, on his death, had been cast out into the Evil Forest. Nwoye joins a sect that has been established in the Evil Forest. Perhaps this suggests to us that the Evil Forest is a place where the Ibos deposit those things by which their society sets no store. Yet, ironically, it is from there that their ultimate salvation will come.

Obierika

Obierika counterparts Okonkwo quite differently from Unoka and Nwoye. No one can accuse him of being weakly or a coward. The first time we see them together, in Chapter 8, Obierika says, 'I am not afraid of blood.' But he is a man who thinks, a man who will obey the law—but not blindly: 'If the Oracle said that my son should be killed I would neither dispute it nor be the one to do it.' Indeed, while he feels that the law should not be broken, he is of the opinion that if a law is unreasonable then it should be changed. In discussing the law that says that a man of the *ozo* title should not climb tall palm trees but is permitted to tap the short ones, he says, 'It is like Dimaragana, who would not lend his knife for cutting up dog-meat because the dog was taboo to him, but offered to use his teeth.' Although he does not know what to do about the established order of things when he feels it to be wrong, he nevertheless questions it. After the disaster of Chapter 13 which brings about Okonkwo's exile, his questionings are made clear:

> Obierika was a man who thought about things. When the will of the goddess had been done, he sat down in his *obi* and mourned his friend's calamity. Why should a man suffer so grievously for an offence he had committed inadvertently? But although he thought for a long time he found no answer.

During Okonkwo's exile it is Obierika who looks after his affairs, thus demonstrating his affection; and when he visits Okonkwo to find out how Nwoye has come to join the Christians, he displays his tact—and his knowledge of his friend's character—by asking not Okonkwo but Nwoye's mother. So it is not surprising that it is with Obierika that Okonkwo most openly discusses his reactions to the disasters that have struck the state. Throughout these discussions it is Obierika who is the voice of reason, setting up logical objections to Okonkwo's headstrong and impulsive attitude, as in Chapter 20:

> Our own men and our sons have joined the ranks of the stranger. . . . If we should try to drive out the white men in Umuofia we should find it easy. . . . But what of our own people who are following their way and have been given the power?

And he sees clearly what has happened:

> The white man is very clever. He came quietly and peaceably with his religion. We were amused at his foolishness and allowed him to stay. Now he has won our brothers, and our clan can no longer act like one. He has put a knife on the things that held us together and we have fallen apart.

This is Okonkwo's far-seeing friend, the man who speaks his grief-stricken epitaph. Like Unoka and Nwoye, he displays in his own way yet another aspect of the Ibo character—thoughtful and perceptive, seeing how men's faiths must adjust to new circumstances and not bring destruction by blind adherence to the old ways.

Themes

If the tale is what happens in the novel, the theme is what it is about. While the theme must of necessity include the tale, it is also something much wider and deeper than merely the story and how it is expressed through character and plot. It is the wider circumstances which lie behind the story and may include the author's purpose in writing it. While there is usually one main theme, there are often minor themes or lesser threads going to make up the whole.

Undoubtedly, the main theme of *Things Fall Apart* is that of change. This change is considered as it affects one society when it comes under pressure from dramatically new ideas—new ideas in religion, in law, in political, economic and social structure. These pressures have occurred often in history, not only when a relatively primitive society has been invaded by the forces of 'civilisation' but also when, for example, a country has changed its political system (as in revolution) or when, say, an agriculture-based economy has changed to one based on industrialisation. When these big changes come about, stresses are set up in society which affect every individual living in that society. Achebe has chosen to consider such changes as they affect the society he knows best, that of his Ibo grandparents, and in so doing he has created a picture that, with minor changes, has been seen in dozens of parts of the world (but perhaps particularly in Africa) over the past century. Thus the interest of his novel for the reader is widened out beyond a consideration of a small corner of West Africa.

When such changes take place one of the almost inevitable results is violence, to a lesser or greater degree. The tragedy of Okonkwo is one expression of that violence. Though his tragedy will, purely by chance, be recorded as a minor footnote in a history-book, we know that there must have been many similar tragedies that have gone unrecorded when similar intransigent characters have tried to oppose change. He merely records impartially what happened, without assigning blame. Ibo traditional society contained a great deal of violence, senseless except in terms of Ibo beliefs, as is amply recorded in the novel, and it is a hope for an end to this violence that sends Nwoye to seek better things in the new order. But the new order establishes and maintains itself by its own kind of violence, and Achebe does not suggest that this new violence is any better than the old: it is merely based on a different view of the world. Ibo law killed for religious reasons, on the command of the God or Oracle: the white man killed according to the commands of a man-based and man-designed structure of laws. Achebe does not say that the latter is better, but he perhaps implies that it ought to be. The manifestations of each type and what happens when they come into collision are presented as facts, re-created and brought alive in fiction.

In Chapter 21, with the discussion between Mr Brown, the missionary, and Akunna, Achebe makes the two religions, Ibo and Christian, confront each other. In what is one of the most wry and pointed passages in the novel, Akunna with his sound common sense and Ibo theology is more than a match for the Christian evangelist with all his book-learning, and he makes it clear that, at base, there is really very little difference between the two faiths. This treatment of the two religions is typical of Achebe's impartial treatment of the two very different cultures throughout the novel.

We might expect that, dealing with such a theme as the sudden change that came over traditional African society with the coming of the white man, Achebe might have had something to say directly on the matter of colonialism, particularly on this subject as a source for all present-day Africa's ills. In essays and lectures he has shown that he has plenty of views on the matter. In *Things Fall Apart*, however, he is silent, preferring to present the facts as they happened, without taking sides, and leaving his readers to make their own deductions. It would be a very biased reader indeed who deduced from this novel that what happened was for the worst. Some of it was good, some of it was bad, but it happened and it was inevitable. Society as it had hitherto existed in Iboland was bound to be annihilated. Achebe's interest—and it is the interest of the true novelist—is in the effect it had upon living, breathing human beings.

This brings us to the second major theme in the novel, which is involved with the very strong and extremely detailed picture given of Ibo life and society prior to the coming of the white man. Some critics, particularly in Europe, have found a somewhat heavy concentration upon what they call 'anthropological detail' in the novel, as if the book were mainly concerned with giving us a picture of how this strange and distant people, so far from what we know as civilisation, lived.

It is necessary that the traditional Ibo society should be displayed in detail and in its entirety since the main theme of the novel is how this society is annihilated. That is why the white man does not come on the scene until two-thirds of the way through the novel. Achebe gives us the detailed account of Ibo life not for its own sake but in order to transport us in our imaginations to this whole society, so that we can readily accept the characters as real, as people we know and understand. Thus it is important for us to know how Okonkwo takes snuff, how he greets his friends, how they converse and the background of beliefs against which all their activities take place. We have to feel we are actually there, transported in time and in place. That is what makes the difference between a novel and a work of social anthropology: though Okonkwo and his fellows never lived, we feel sure that this is how it must really have been.

There is still another reason why the Ibo background is treated in so much detail in the novel. This is tied in with the undercurrent of nostalgia that runs through the book as a minor theme. Nostalgia is a regretful longing for things that are past. It is often sad and regretful as if suggesting that things were better in the old days. However, Achebe's nostalgia is not of this sentimental sort. In part, it is a natural effect of his detailed and realistic treatment of the past, and in part a result of his desire to present things as they really were. He does not suggest that the old days and ways were better—though Okonkwo thinks they were —but he does wish to present them whole. His overriding desire in the novel is to establish this Ibo society as a *reality*.

There are several reasons why he wishes to do this. For a start, he knows that many of his readers will not have the slightest idea of what such a society was like. Therefore, everything that such readers learn about it must be contained within the novel itself and must not be dependent upon knowledge of history and the like brought from outside. This is why it is hardly necessary to give elaborate notes on Ibo customs and beliefs: everything is explained to us, in the simplest way, as we read. So this society, strange and foreign as it might be, comes alive to us and we are able to see these Ibo tribesmen as human beings, since we are looking at them 'from the inside', as it were. We have only to imagine, for example, how different the events of Part Three would be were we to see them from the point of view of the missionaries or the District Commissioner.

Secondly, though the circumstances of the story will be much more familiar to his African readers, he has to make them clear even to such a readership. As it has turned out, with the tremendous development of literacy and education in Africa over the past twenty years, the majority of his readers have, in fact, been African. For them, Achebe has had to create a past, bedded in historical reality, which they can understand and of which they can feel proud. At one time, educated by colonial masters, many Africans were inclined to despise their past. They knew about Greece and Rome, they knew about British history, but the past of their own nations, their African heritage, was a blank to them or was viewed as a dark night of barbarism and savagery. *Things Fall Apart* shows them what this past must have been like, thus explaining how the present came about in a way no European history books could, displaying the great deal that was good in African traditional society that was swept aside in the tide of history—ideas, in particular, of kinship and community and democracy—and giving them a past of which they can be truly proud and unashamed.

However, while in part a writer's intention in writing a novel is to communicate his ideas to his readers, often his first, and unrecognised, desire is to work things out and explain them to himself. This, one cannot help feeling, Achebe has done for himself in *Things Fall Apart*, creating a past for himself and his people that has a living reality greater than his own actual, if largely unknown, past. In so doing, he has created a past for all Africans and—perhaps more splendidly and importantly—created a living past for his people in the eyes of the whole outside world.

Language and style

Things Fall Apart is written in the simplest of simple sentences, short and terse, which seem to fall down one after the other like beads upon a string. The linkages between the sentences are linkages of sense, not grammatical links, and there is no attempt to join the statements together into complicated and flowing sentences. If you take the first paragraph of the book and write out the first five sentences separately, this becomes clear:

(1) Okonkwo was well known throughout the nine villages and even beyond.
(2) His fame rested on solid personal achievements.
(3) As a young man of eighteen he had brought honour to his village by throwing Amalinze the Cat.
(4) Amalinze was the great wrestler who for seven years was unbeaten, from Umuofia to Mbaino.
(5) He was called the Cat because his back would never touch the earth.

The ideas that make one sentence lead to another are: *fame* (1 to 2), *achievement* (2 to 3), *Amalinze* (3 to 4), *Cat* (4 to 5).

A possible rewriting of this passage in more complex sentences might be:

Okonkwo, whose fame rested on solid personal achievements, was well known throughout the nine villages and beyond, since as a young man of eighteen he had brought honour to his village by throwing Amalinze the Cat. Amalinze, who was called the Cat because his back would never touch the earth, was the great wrestler who for seven years was unbeaten from Umuofia to Mbaino.

Achebe seems determined to write not just in simple sentences but in short sentences. On the third page of the novel, for example, very minor alterations in punctuation and so on would present the same words in longer sentences:

(1) Okoye was also a musician.
(2) He played on the *ogene*.
(3) But he was not a failure like Unoka.
(4) He had a large barn full of yams and he had three wives.
(5) And now he was going to take the Idemili title, the third highest in the land.
(6) It was a very expensive ceremony and he was gathering all his resources together.
(7) That was in fact the reason why he had come to see Unoka.

> Okoye was also a musician who played upon the *ogene* but who was not a failure like Unoka and had a large barn full of yams and three wives. Now he was going to take the Idemili title, the third highest in the land, which was a very expensive ceremony, so he was gathering his resources together and that was in fact the reason he had come to see Unoka.

The reason Achebe writes in this way is not because he is unable to write in a more complex and sophisticated way but because he wishes the style of the novel to be in accord with the rest of his story and subject matter. The effect that the style creates is a subtle one. It suggests first of all that we are in a simpler age than today and, secondly, that it is perhaps being *spoken* by a narrator. The spoken language in everyday use is normally made up of simple sentences and statements and not of highly complex and involved sentences. Thirdly, it suggests perhaps that it is being spoken in the Ibo language, whose structures are simpler than those of twentieth-century English. The world he is describing is the Ibo world, and the 'tone of voice' in which he is writing (which is another way of saying 'style') is that of an Ibo man.

For the same reason, all the words he uses are of the simplest and are such as would be used in the Ibo world of which he is writing. There are no long and complicated words, no difficult abstract words and not a single word that tastes of the twentieth century. The images used are also entirely of the Ibo world, as are the comparisons and similes — though the latter are rare:

Okonkwo's fame had grown like a bush-fire in the harmattan. (Chapter 1)

[Ikemefuna] grew rapidly like a yam tendril in the rainy season. (Chapter 7)

The oldest man present said sternly that those whose palm-kernels were cracked for them by a benevolent spirit should not forget to be humble. (Chapter 4)

. . . a lot of effeminate men clucking like old hens. (Chapter 17)

He has put a knife on the things that held us together and we have fallen apart. (Chapter 20)

The simplicity of the words used, when combined with imagery and references that are strictly limited to the world and concerns of the forest tribesman of the end of last century, reinforces strongly the simplicity of the sentences and creates the impression that we are totally immersed in the life and affairs of Umuofia. It is as if we were listening to the story being told by an anonymous tribesman of the period. This impression is heightened by Achebe's use of proverbs.

Proverbs, which are pithy, wise sayings which embody some supposed truth or moral lesson, are found in all languages, and their wisdom is usually a simple and practical folk wisdom which one feels has been handed down from generation to generation by word of mouth. Examples of such sayings in English are: 'A stitch in time saves nine'; 'Every cloud has a silver lining'; 'Least said, soonest mended'; there are many hundreds more. But in complex civilisations which have come to depend upon the printed book for the transmission of wisdom from generation to generation, such sayings have fallen out of favour and are often only used jocularly or, orally, to point some particularly appropriate circumstances.

However, in societies which are non-literate, and in the simpler peasant societies, proverbs persist and form a handy everyday anthology of the wisdom of the society. In the Ibo-land of *Things Fall Apart* they have been developed into a highly approved adornment and embellishment of formal speech. As we have seen, the ornamental language, the many elaborate figures of speech and the tricks of rhetoric common in languages that have been written down for a long time are all absent from Ibo speech. Instead we have proverbs—sayings which are memorable and which will thus hook on to the mind when complex metaphors and arrangements of syntax have been forgotten. The stylistic hallmark of Ibo speech is the use of the proverb. The trick, particularly in formal speech, is to bring in as many proverbs as possible and to use them as appropriately as possible; and the speaker who can do this well is the one who will gain most approval from his audience. Sometimes, also, proverbs are used as a form of politeness, merely hinting at what one does not like to say openly—as when, in Chapter 1, Okoye is trying to persuade Unoka to return him the two hundred cowries he had borrowed:

> Having spoken plainly so far, Okoye said the next half a dozen sentences in proverbs. Among the Ibo the art of conversation is regarded very highly, and proverbs are the palm-oil with which words are eaten.

In other words, proverbs can be used to lubricate social relationships. And it is worthy of notice that Unoka eases himself out of this awkward position by using a proverb:

> Our elders say that the sun will shine on those who stand before it shines on those who kneel under them. I shall pay my big debts first.

The Ibo proverbs are, of course, drawn from the Ibo experience or the Ibo religious beliefs:

> If a child washed his hands he could eat with kings. (Chapter 1)
> The lizard that jumped from the high iroko tree to the ground said he would praise himself if no one else did. (Chapter 3)
> Eneke the bird says that since men have learnt to shoot without missing, he has learnt to fly without perching. (Chapter 3)

> They called him [Okonkwo] the little bird *nza* who so far forgot himself after a heavy meal that he challenged his *chi*. (Chapter 4)

Each of these proverbs is brought in aptly to accord with the circumstances it is commenting on, be it Okonkwo's achievements or his pride or Nwakibie's stinginess with his yams.

Often the proverbs merge with and blend into references to the folk tales and legends of the Ibo, just as in English literature there are often references to a common stock of classical mythology. Every Ibo tribesman would know these stories:

> It is like Dimaragana, who would not lend his knife for cutting up dog-meat because the dog was taboo to him, but offered to use his teeth. (Chapter 8)

Sometimes, also, these anecdotes are quite lengthy, but they always have a purpose in the story. Thus the tale of Mosquito and Ear is at the beginning of Chapter 9 in which Ezinma falls ill with malaria and the tale of Mother Kite in Chapter 15 warns against attacking before knowing the strength of one's enemy; and the long tale of Tortoise and the birds that opens Chapter 11 not only serves the purpose of creating the peaceful atmosphere of a mother telling her child a bed-time story, making what happens thereafter all the more frightening, but also tells us much of the moral quality of a society that condemns greed and acquisitiveness.

The use of proverbs and folk tales is yet another way in which Achebe adds truth to the Ibo atmosphere of the novel. To have omitted them, or to have used extensively the tricks and flourishes of more advanced written languages, would have created a very different book, a book in which both the author and we as readers would be looking at Ibo society from the outside. As it is, the use of proverbs and anecdote, along with the simple sentence-structure and the use of words and images restricted to the Ibo experience, means that Achebe's style makes a significant contribution to the novel as a whole. This is what style must do. 'Style' is not the use of elaborate and ornamental languages and forms. It is the most effective use of language for the author's purpose. And Achebe's purpose is to re-create in entirety the vanished world of *Things Fall Apart*.

Part 4

Hints for study

Reading and study

The first time you read a novel you will read it fairly swiftly in order to understand the story. This is, after all, what the writer intended, and he has so arranged the material of the story in a plot in such a way as to capture your interest and maintain your attention. You are reading for recreation, in order to be transported out of yourself and into the world and circumstances of the tale. Although you may pause and re-read a little occasionally or look up the meaning of a word in the dictionary or perhaps, in the case of *Things Fall Apart*, in the glossary of Ibo words, you will be reading fairly uncritically and for enjoyment, surrendering yourself to the skill of the writer. Apart from understanding the simple meaning of what is said, you will be contented with appreciating the tale.

For most novels you read you will never go further than this. If, however, you wish to study the book—particularly if you are studying it for an examination—you will then have to read the book much more closely and critically. The questions that a critical reading of the novel will be asking are the big critical questions, such as: What is the writer doing? How does he do it? Why is he doing it? To what extent does he succeed in achieving his aims? Where does the work, as a whole, fit into the broad category of novels, and what that is new or original does it contribute to the art of the novel? There are, of course, other critical questions that can be asked, and other, more specific and detailed, questions about this particular novel, but these are the sort of broad, general questions that should be at the back of your mind when you turn from reading for enjoyment to reading with a critical sense.

Thus, your second reading will be one that is much more careful and detailed than your first. Read each chapter in turn, with great care, keeping a notebook beside you as you read. Do not leave any chapter until you are quite sure that you understand it fully, since the object of this reading is to make quite sure of your understanding of the *meaning*. As well, as you read, you may find ideas about the book occurring to you—perhaps about the characterisation or the style or the themes. You should capture these stray ideas by writing them down, because, no matter how hard you try, you will never remember them all later on. It is as well, too, to jot down any significant quotations that you come across that might later be of assistance to you when you come to write essays or examination answers on the book.

Do not skimp this particular stage of your study. The chapter-by-chapter summaries given in Part 2 of these Notes are no substitute for your own close reading—particularly for a novel already so terse and condensed as *Things Fall Apart*—but they are useful to refresh your memory or to locate particular incidents quickly and easily.

Having completed this careful reading of the novel, you should now read or re-read Part 3 of these Notes. You should still maintain your practice of jotting down ideas that occur to you as you read, and you will find revision much easier if you make a brief summary (perhaps, even, a simple list of headings or topics) as you read each section. You are now well on the way to 'knowing' the book—an essential preliminary to being able to answer the sort of questions that are asked about it in examinations or to writing essays on its major themes.

At this point it is a good idea to turn away from the book for a few days. During this period you could perhaps learn more about the author (see Part 1 of these Notes), or look at some of his other works. But all the time your inner mind will be working on the material you have assimilated, ordering and organising it within your own store of knowledge about other books and your own experience. From time to time fresh ideas will occur to you—and these too should go into your notebook.

You are now ready for a further reading of the novel. This time, however, you will be reading it against the background of all you have learnt and thought about it previously. Your mind will be much more alive and critically aware of what is going on, and you will find that you are making notes on the various aspects of the novel (plot, characterisation, themes and style) and clarifying your own views and opinions on these matters. Now you will really command a knowledge of the book and will find that in, say, preparing to write an essay, appropriate incidents and examples or quotations will come readily to mind, to be confirmed by turning to selected passages.

Context questions

It is possible that, either in the course of teaching or in some examinations, you will be set what are known as 'context questions'. These are questions in which a short passage from the book, usually of two or three sentences, is given and you are asked to answer certain questions on it. Their purpose is to check that you know the book, are acquainted with the tale and the plot and have understood the passage.

Students are sometimes worried at the prospect of such questions and read and re-read the book in an attempt to assimilate and remember everything. This is quite unnecessary. No one is going to pick out at random a passage from the book and ask you if you can say where it occurs. For example, no one is likely to ask you to locate the following passage:

> Okonkwo's first wife soon finished her cooking and set before their guests a big meal of pounded yams and bitter-leaf soup. Okonkwo's son, Nwoye, brought in a pot of sweet wine tapped from the raffia palm.

What your examiner is interested in is knowing that you have read and understood the main lines of the story. Therefore, the passages he asks you to locate will be significant, notable passages, usually from critical points in the tale. Thus, if you are asked to locate a passage it will be from some key point, such as the murder of Ikemefuna or the death of Okonkwo, or some highlight, such as the judgement of the *egwugwu* or the attack on Mr Smith's mission-church.

Sometimes, however, you will be asked not to identify a passage but to comment on it. What you are being asked for here is a comment on some feature of the novel, perhaps the characterisation, themes or style. Thus, you might be given the following passage:

> But it was really not true that Okonkwo's palm-kernels had been cracked for him by a benevolent spirit. He had cracked them himself. Anyone who knew his grim struggle against poverty and misfortune could not say he had been lucky. If ever a man deserved his success, that man was Okonkwo. At an early age he had achieved fame as the greatest wrestler in all the land. That was not luck. At the most one could say that his *chi* or personal god was good. But the Ibo people have a proverb that when a man says yes his *chi* says yes also. Okonkwo said yes very strongly; so his *chi* agreed. And not only his *chi* but his clan too, because it judged a man by the work of his hands.

The sort of questions you might be asked on this passage would be designed to show that you had an idea of Okonkwo's nature and character. As well, you might be asked to explain the meaning of the proverbs or of the word *chi*. If you try it for yourself, you will see that context questions are really quite difficult to answer and depend on a sound understanding of the novel. A close and careful reading of the book, making sure that you understand everything as you go, coupled with a study of the sections of these Notes dealing with these subjects, will go a long way in helping you to answer such questions.

A moment's thought will tell you in what particular aspect of the book examiner is interested. Suppose the following passage is given:

> Among the Ibo the art of conversation is regarded very highly, and proverbs are the palm-oil with which words are eaten.

The examiner is evidently interested in Achebe's style, in particular his use of proverbs, and, as well as asking for the meaning of the phrase about palm-oil, which is itself a proverb, may ask you for other examples of Ibo proverbs or even, more generally, for a brief note on the nature and use of proverbs in the book.

A good way of practising such questions, and at the same time increasing your knowledge of the book, is to select short passages and to write down what questions you would ask if you wished to test someone else's knowledge.

What sort of questions would you ask on the following passages?

(1) But if the Oracle said that my son should be killed I would neither dispute it nor be the one to do it.

(2) Okonkwo was popularly called the 'Roaring Flame'. As he looked into the log fire he recalled the name. He was a flaming fire. How then could he have begotten a son like Nwoye, degenerate and effeminate? Perhaps he was not his son. No! he could not be. His wife had played him false. He would teach her! But Nwoye resembled his grandfather, Unoka, who was Okonkwo's father. He pushed the thought out of his mind. He, Okonkwo, was called a flaming fire. How could he have begotten a woman for a son? At Nwoye's age Okonkwo had already become famous throughout Umuofia for his wrestling and his fearlessness.

(3) But I fear for you young people because you do not understand how strong is the bond of kinship. You do not know what it is to speak with one voice. And what is the result? An abominable religion has settled among you. A man can now leave his father and his brothers. He can curse the gods of his fathers and his ancestors, like a hunter's dog that suddenly goes mad and turns on his master. I fear for you; I fear for the clan.

(4) Okonkwo did as the priest said. He also took with him a pot of palm-wine. Inwardly, he was repentant. But he was not the man to go about telling his neighbours that he was in error. And so people said he had no respect for the gods of the clan. His enemies said his good fortune had gone to his head.

In answering such questions, do not try to re-tell the whole story, but give the circumstances briefly in your own words. Do not be afraid to refer to matters outside the given passage, which will show that you understand the whole novel. And remember to answer in complete sentences and not in one-word answers.

Essays and examination questions

Writing essays and examination answers are really the same sort of task under different conditions, since examination answers are just short essays.

The most important thing is to read the question carefully and make sure you understand it, since you must try to answer the question that is asked—not the question you think is asked, or the question you would like to have been asked and have prepared for! If you read carefully you will see that, as with context questions, the examiner is concerned with one specific aspect of the book, one of the aspects that have been dealt with in these Notes.

Very occasionally you will be asked to tell some major incident in your own words—for example, an account of what happened to Ikemefuna. Here you should use your own words and make your answer short enough to be answered in the time at your disposal. Such questions are, however, rare in examinations and are more likely to be set by a teacher wishing to be sure you know the story. More common is the question which you *think* may be answered by re-telling the story or a part of it. It is always wrong to think a question can be answered by re-telling the story. A question is always answered by a reasoned reply, an analysis or an argument, and a mere reference to the story is all that is called for.

More students fail for not answering the question asked or for simply re-telling the story than for any other cause—except writing in incoherent English with chaotic grammar and syntax. So beware! ANSWER THE QUESTION.

Some questions will deal with *characterisation*:

(1) 'Okonkwo never showed any emotions openly, unless it be the emotion of anger.' Discuss Okonkwo's character in the light of this quotation.

(2) 'His whole life was dominated by fear, the fear of failure and of weakness.' Do you think this is true of Okonkwo? If so, explain how this came about and say if you think it an adequate summary of his character.

(3) Compare and contrast the characters of Okonkwo and Obierika.

To answer such questions it is well to have worked out brief (300–500-word) studies of the principal characters (Okonkwo, Unoka, Obierika, Nwoye) and to study the section on characters in Part 3 of these Notes.

Sometimes you will be asked to discuss 'the part played' by such-and-such a character in the novel; for example, 'Discuss the part played by Unoka in the novel.' Remember this question is not asking you to give an account of what Unoka does or what happens to him, but an account of his effect upon the other characters and upon the story. Thus, the nature of Unoka, and his example, goes a long way to explaining Okonkwo's character and his attitude later on towards Nwoye, whom he sees as mirroring his own father in reproducing the Ibo virtues which he despises.

Some questions deal with *style*:

(1) Describe Achebe's style of writing in this novel, with examples, and say why you think it is well fitted to the story.

(2) Discuss, with examples, the use of proverbs in this novel.

More difficult questions are those which deal, directly or indirectly, with *themes*:

(1) What do you think are the main themes in *Things Fall Apart*?
(2) 'One of the main themes of *Things Fall Apart* is that of change.' Discuss the ways in which this theme is illustrated in the plotting of the novel.
(3) In a description of the characteristics of Ibo society prior to the coming of the white man, say why you think Achebe has drawn such a detailed picture in *Things Fall Apart*.
(4) Using evidence drawn from *Things Fall Apart*, would you say that Achebe has a longing for 'the good old days'?

The most difficult questions of all are those which require you to make up your own mind, on evidence drawn from the book, about the correct answer. Sometimes two alternative possibilities are presented to you, sometimes you are asked for a view. The important thing to remember here is that your arguments should always be supported by evidence from the book, by references or by quotations. Often such questions will require you to use your total knowledge of the book, not just your knowledge of one or two aspects.

(1) Do you think it is correct to say that Okonkwo commits suicide 'to escape the results of his rash courage against the white man'?

Here your knowledge not only of the story but also of Okonkwo's character and of one of the main themes of the book will come into play around the main thread of a question that is really asking: 'Why does Okonkwo commit suicide?'

(2) 'Achebe merely records impartially what happened, without assigning blame.' Do you agree with this statement? Attempt in your answer to give reasons for Achebe's attitude to his material.

This is a question that will test to the utmost your knowledge of the book and your answer will show your understanding of what Achebe has attempted and what he has achieved. In considering your answer you should ask yourself such questions as: Can the characters be grouped into good characters and bad characters? Do you think all was ideal in the old Ibo society? Why do you think the white man does not appear until Chapter 15? What do you think is the effect of the final paragraph of the novel? Would the book have been different if Okonkwo had not hanged himself?

(3) '*Things Fall Apart*—the tragedy of an individual or the tragedy of a society?' Discuss.

At first sight this question seems to offer a simple alternative to which you should give a firm answer on one side or the other. On reflection, however, you may feel that the matter is more complex than this. Is it not perhaps the case that Achebe has used the story of what happened to one tribesman of a particular character to illustrate what happened to Ibo society at the critical moment of the coming of the white man? And is what happened to Ibo society properly described as a 'tragedy', however we may describe what happened to Okonkwo? Be particularly careful, in answering such open and general questions, to support your discussion with references to incidents and with quotations. The main points to remember in writing essays are:

(1) Read the question carefully and be sure you understand precisely what it means.
(2) After reflection, in the light of your knowledge of the book, make up your mind in general terms about what your answer will be.
(3) Construct a skeleton-plan of headings in which your arguments are marshalled one after another in an order which leads to your conclusion. This will give shape and order to your essay.
(4) It is often useful to write a first paragraph in which you state concisely what you are going to do in the essay and how you are going to do it. This will probably not be included in your completed essay.
(5) Find examples, incidents and quotations to support the various steps of your argument.
(6) Write a first draft.
(7) Work carefully through your draft, paying particular attention to links between paragraphs and sentences so that your whole composition *flows*.
(8) Write out your essay in its final form.

In an examination, because your draft will in fact be your final answer, you will need to be very careful over it and take especial pains with your skeleton-plan. If you know the book thoroughly and have studied these Notes diligently, your problem will not be finding something to say but knowing what to leave out.

Part 5

Suggestions for further reading

The text

Things Fall Apart, first published by Heinemann, London, in their 'African Writers Series' in 1958, has been reprinted several times. The edition currently available, first published in 1967, has a biographical note, a glossary of the Ibo words and phrases used and four-line-drawings.

Other works by Chinua Achebe

No Longer At Ease (1960), *Arrow of God* (1964; revised edition, 1974) and *A Man of the People* (1966) are all published by Heinemann Educational Books, London, in their 'African Writers Series', and this is the order in which the novels are best read (after *Things Fall Apart* has itself been read). The short stories, *Girls at War* (1971), and the poems, *Beware Soul Brother* (1972), are also available in the same series.

Morning Yet on Creation Day, Heinemann, London, 1975, a collection of Achebe's essays, contains several items helpful for an understanding of his work.

Criticism

Most critical essays on Achebe have appeared in magazines that are difficult to obtain. More readily obtainable are:

RAVENSCROFT, ARTHUR: *Chinua Achebe*, Longman, London, 1969 (Writers and their Work, No. 209); the best, and cheapest, introduction.

KILLAM, D.G.: *The Novels of Chinua Achebe*, Heinemann, London, 1969; a serious work for the most advanced students.

The author of these notes

T.A. DUNN was educated at the University of Edinburgh; he has been Professor of English Studies in the University of Stirling since its foundation in 1966. Before that he spent twelve years in West Africa where he was Professor of English in the University of Ghana and then first Professor of English in the University of Lagos. He came to Stirling after a year as Visiting Professor in the University of Western Ontario, Canada.

The University of Ghana was the first university to introduce the study of African literature in English into undergraduate courses, and similarly in Stirling Professor Dunn has fostered this study as one of his Department's special interests. He is a personal friend of Chinua Achebe who has been awarded an Honorary Doctorate of the University of Stirling.

Professor Dunn's main interest is in drama and the theatre, and he has published a study of the Jacobean playwright, Philip Massinger, as well as an edition of *The Fatal Dowry* by Massinger and Field. For some years he was editor of a West African literary quarterly, *Universitas*, and, in addition, he is (with D.E.S. Maxwell) the author of *Introducing Poetry*.

York Handbooks: list of titles

YORK HANDBOOKS form a companion series to York Notes and are designed to meet the wider needs of students of English and related fields. Each volume is a compact study of a given subject area, written by an authority with experience in communicating the essential ideas to students at all levels.

AN A.B.C. OF SHAKESPEARE
by P. C. BAYLEY

A DICTIONARY OF BRITISH AND IRISH AUTHORS
by ANTONY KAMM

A DICTIONARY OF LITERARY TERMS (Second Edition)
by MARTIN GRAY

ENGLISH GRAMMAR
by LORETO TODD

ENGLISH POETRY
by CLIVE T. PROBYN

AN INTRODUCTION TO AUSTRALIAN LITERATURE
by TREVOR JAMES

AN INTRODUCTION TO LINGUISTICS
by LORETO TODD

AN INTRODUCTION TO LITERARY CRITICISM
by RICHARD DUTTON

AN INTRODUCTORY GUIDE TO ENGLISH LITERATURE
by MARTIN STEPHEN

THE METAPHYSICAL POETS
by TREVOR JAMES

PREPARING FOR EXAMINATIONS IN ENGLISH LITERATURE
by NEIL McEWAN

READING THE SCREEN: AN INTRODUCTION TO FILM STUDIES
by JOHN IZOD

STUDYING CHAUCER
by ELISABETH BREWER

STUDYING JANE AUSTEN
by IAN MILLIGAN

STUDYING SHAKESPEARE
by MARTIN STEPHEN *and* PHILIP FRANKS

STUDYING THOMAS HARDY
by LANCE ST JOHN BUTLER

WOMEN WRITERS IN ENGLISH LITERATURE
by JANE STEVENSON